HARLEQUIN®
Presents~

At Harlequin Presents we are always interested in what you, the readers, think about the series. So if you have any thoughts you'd like to share, please join in the discussion of your favorite books at www.iheartpresents.com—created by and for fans of Harlequin Presents!

On the site, find blog entries written by authors and fans, the inside scoop from editors and links to authors and books. Enjoy and share with others the unique world of Presents— we'd love to hear from you!

Bedded by...

Blackmail

Forced to bed...then to wed?

He's got her firmly in his sights and she's got only one chance of survival—surrender to his blackmail...and him...in his bed!

Bedded by... Blackmail

The *big* miniseries from Harlequin Presents®.

Dare you read it?

Julia James

THE ITALIAN'S RAGS-TO-RICHES WIFE

Bedded by... *Blackmail*
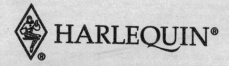
Forced to bed...then to wed?

◆ **HARLEQUIN**®

TORONTO • NEW YORK • LONDON
AMSTERDAM • PARIS • SYDNEY • HAMBURG
STOCKHOLM • ATHENS • TOKYO • MILAN • MADRID
PRAGUE • WARSAW • BUDAPEST • AUCKLAND

ISBN-13: 978-0-373-12716-0
ISBN-10:   0-373-12716-2

THE ITALIAN'S RAGS-TO-RICHES WIFE

First North American Publication 2008.

All about the author...
Julia James

JULIA JAMES lives in England with her family. Harlequin® novels were the first "grown-up" books she read as a teenager, alongside Georgette Heyer and Daphne du Maurier, and she's been reading them ever since. Julia adores the British countryside—in all its seasons—and is fascinated by all things historical, from castles to cottages. She also has a special love for the Mediterranean—"the most perfect landscape after England!" She considers both ideal settings for romance stories. Since becoming a romance writer, she has, she says, had the great good fortune to start discovering the Caribbean, as well, and is happy to report that those magical, beautiful islands are also ideal settings for romance stories. "One of the best things about writing romance is that it gives you a great excuse to take holidays in fabulous places," says Julia, "all in the name of research, of course!"

Her first stab at novel writing was Regency romances. "But, alas, no one wanted to publish them," she says. She put her writing aside until her family commitments were clear, and then renewed her love affair with contemporary romances. "My writing partner and I made a pact not to give up until we were published—and we both succeeded! Natasha Oakley writes for Harlequin Romance®, and we faithfully read each other's works in progress and give each other a lot of free advice and encouragement."

In between writing Julia enjoys walking, gardening, needlework, baking "extremely gooey chocolate cakes" and trying to stay fit!

PROLOGUE

'WHAT do you mean, you're retaining the chairmanship?'

The voice that had spoken was harsh, and clearly angry. But out of respect for the man he had addressed, a man more than twice his age, Allesandro di Vincenzo kept the anger under control.

'The situation has changed,' the other man replied sombrely. He was sitting in his leather chair, in the library of his eighteenth-century villa in the depths of the Roman countryside.

Allesandro drew in his breath sharply. His lithe body was clad in a handmade suit from one of Italy's most stylish and fashionable designers, and his sable feathered hair was superbly cut, setting off a face whose features could have graced an Italian movie star, let alone the chief executive of a major Italian company. He had dark, long-lashed eyes, high cheekbones, a finely cut nose, planed jaw and a sculpted, mobile mouth which, at the moment, was drawn in a taut, forbidding line.

'But it's been understood you would step down in my favour—'

'Only by you, Allesandro,' the older man retorted. 'I never gave any legally binding undertaking. You simply assumed that when Stefano died—' His voice broke off a moment, then he recovered, and continued. 'And, as I have said, the situation has changed. Changed in a way I could never have envisaged.'

For a moment the sombre look left him, and he shook his head, looking suddenly every one of his seventy years.

'I could have had no idea—none at all…' His voice trailed off.

Allesandro's brows drew together impatiently. His long-fingered hands pushed back his jacket, indenting around his lean hips.

'What is this, Tomaso? No idea about what?'

The old man looked at him again. He paused a moment before speaking, his voice heavy.

'Stefano hid it from me completely. I discovered it now, only when I was able to face going through his personal effects. What I found shocked me to the core.' He paused again, as if collecting himself, then continued, still in the same heavy voice.

'The letters are over twenty-five years old—why he kept them I do not know. It cannot have been sentimental attachment, for the last of them says that it will be the final letter—that the writer accepts, finally, that Stefano will not reply. But for whatever reason they survived. And the fact that they did—' his gaze rested unreadably on the younger man again '—changes everything.'

Allesandro's expression was closed.

'How so?' he prompted. There was wariness in his voice, and suspicion. The old man was being evasive, and Allesandro was running out of patience. Ever since Tomaso's forty-five-year-old son, Stefano, doggedly bachelor, had smashed himself up in his power-boat ten months ago, Allesandro had been earmarked to move up from being the energetic and highly successful chief executive of the company founded by his late father and Tomaso Viale to being chairman of Viale-Vincenzo—with full control. He had given Tomaso time to mourn—even though his relations with his son had never been good—and had even accepted Tomaso taking on the temporary role of caretaker chairman after the initial shock of Stefano's death.

But enough was enough. Tomaso had given Allesandro every reason to expect that he would retire before the end of the financial year and hand full control of the company over to him. Frustration bit at Allesandro. He had places to be, things to do, plans to execute—and having to make the journey here had *not* been on his agenda. *Dio*, he could think of a dozen places he'd rather be right now. Starting with the Rome apartment of Delia Dellatore, whose voluptuous charms were currently exclusively reserved solely for his enjoyment.

He threw a covertly assessing look at Tomaso and saw that he had aged since Stefano's death. Stefano might not have been a satisfactory son—his flamboyant playboy lifestyle had been wild and self-indulgent—but his death had been a devastating shock.

And now it seemed Tomaso had suffered yet another shock—sufficient enough to distract him from the business of the chairmanship of Viale-Vincenzo.

'How so, Tomaso?' Allesandro prompted again. Whatever it was that was keeping the chairmanship out of his reach, he wanted it sorted.

Tomaso's eyes had a strange expression as he looked at Allesandro before speaking.

'As you know, Stefano refused to marry, preferring his wild lifestyle.' There was a familiar disapproval in Tomaso's voice. 'So I had little hope of the continuation of my line. But those letters I found were from a woman. A young Englishwoman imploring Stefano to come to her, to at least acknowledge her letters. And her reason for writing them…'

He paused again, and Allesandro saw emotion in the lined face.

'She bore Stefano a child. A daughter. My granddaughter.' His hands tightened over the cusp of the arms of the leather chair. He looked straight at the younger man.

'I want you to find her and bring her here to me, Allesandro.'

CHAPTER ONE

LAURA braced her shoulders and lifted the handles of the overladen wheelbarrow. The tower of damp kindling she had gathered wobbled a moment, but did not fall. Blinking the rain from her eyelashes, she set off over the bumpy ground of the orchard towards the gate that led into the back yard. Her rubber boots swished through the long, wet grass, and her worn corduroy trousers were damp, as was her baggy jacket and hood, but it didn't bother her. She was used to the rain. It rained a lot in the West Country. Gaining the Tarmacked surface of the back yard made her progress easier, and she headed for the woodshed. Firewood was valuable, and helped cut down on expensive oil and electricity bills.

She needed to save every penny she could.

Not just for the essential repairs to the house which, even when her grandparents had been alive, had become increasingly neglected due to shortage of cash, but also, now that she had inherited Wharton, to pay off the death duties that the taxman had imposed on her.

Anxiety bit at her. Even as her head told her that selling Wharton was the most sensible course of action, her heart rebelled vehemently. She couldn't just sell it like a pair of old shoes!

It was the only home she could remember—her haven from the world. She had been brought up in its sheltering protection by her grandparents after the sorry and shameful tragedy that had befallen their only daughter. A daughter who had died, unmarried, and left behind an illegitimate baby…with a father who had refused to acknowledge her.

But there was no income to go with Wharton. Laura's only hope of keeping it was to convert it to an upmarket holiday let— but that required a new kitchen, *en suite* bathrooms, extensive repairs and redecorating. All far too expensive.

Worse, the first tranche of tax was due imminently, and her only means of paying it was by selling the last few paintings and antiques she had in the house. Laura hated the idea of selling them, but was faced with no other option.

Anxiety pressed her again, a constant companion.

As she emptied her barrowload of kindling into the woodshed to dry off, and set off back towards the orchard to gather yet more, she halted suddenly. A car was approaching down the long drive from the road.

Few people ever called. Her grandparents had kept themselves very much to themselves, and Laura did likewise. As she listened, she heard the car take the fork to the seldom-used front drive. Abandoning the wheelbarrow, she set off around the side of the house.

A gleaming silver saloon car was pulled up outside the front door, its sides flecked with mud but still looking as sleek and expensive and as out of place as if it had been a spaceship.

And looking even more out of place was the man who was getting out of it.

Laura's mouth fell open, and she stared gormlessly, blinking in the rain.

Allesandro stepped out of the car, his expression taut, barely suppressing his black mood. Even with SatNav the narrow, winding lanes had been almost impossible to navigate. And now that he was finally here the place seemed deserted. The stone surface of the old house was as damp and sodden as the landscape that surrounded him. Broken, dirty shutters blanked out the downstairs windows and the drive was green with weeds. The flowerbeds looked windswept and unkempt, and the ancient rhododendrons crowded the sides of the overgrown lawn. There was a piece of guttering hanging loose and spilling rainwater onto the porch, which was crumbling.

Ducking through the rain, he gained the relative cover of the entrance. It had been raining solidly ever since his landing at Exeter, and showed no signs of stopping. Allesandro's dark eyes flashed disparagingly as he took in the dilapidated state of the house. Was it really as deserted as it looked?

The crunch of trodden gravel made him swivel his head.

No, not deserted.

Some kind of outdoor hand, he assumed, was approaching him, clumping in heavy boots, the bulky figure enveloped in a worn waxed coat and concealing hood.

'Is Miss Stowe in?' he demanded, raising his voice through the rain.

Laura Stowe. That was the name of Stefano's daughter. Her mother, so Allesandro's investigations had uncovered, had been Susan Stowe, and Stefano had met her while she had been an art student visiting Italy. Apparently Susan had been pretty, and naïve, and the results had been predictable. Allesandro had also discovered that Susan Stowe had died when her daughter was three, and the child had been raised by her maternal grandparents, here in this house.

At least, Allesandro thought grimly, the girl would be overjoyed to discover she had a rich grandfather wanting to take her in. This place was a derelict dump.

His mood was bad. He didn't want to be here, practically as Tomaso's gofer, but Tomaso had indicated that once he had met his granddaughter, he would want to retire, to have more time with her. That suited Allesandro perfectly.

What did not suit him was being kept out in the cold and the wet.

'Miss Stowe?' he repeated impatiently. 'Is she in?'

The bulky figure spoke suddenly.

'I'm Laura Stowe. What was it you wanted?'

Allesandro stared disbelievingly. '*You* are Laura Stowe?' he said.

* * *

The expression on the visitor's face might have made her laugh, but Laura was too taken aback by his presence to find it humorous. What on earth was someone like this doing here—and of all things looking for *her*? Someone who was not just utterly out of place here, but—she swallowed silently—who was just jaw-droppingly good-looking. Night-dark hair, night-dark eyes, and a face cut with the same chisel Michelangelo must have used. His skin had a natural tan to it, she registered, and as for his clothes...

They went with the swish car; that was obvious. They screamed designer—from the superb fit across his shoulders to the pristine whiteness of his shirt, the crisp elegance of his tie and the lean length of his trousered legs and the polish on his leather shoes. These clothes had not been made in England—not even by a top Savile Row tailor.

They were as foreign as he was.

The final element clicked into place. It was his voice, she realised. It was accented. Perfect, but accented. Italian, she thought, her brain still reeling. That was what he looked like. And even as the word gelled in her head, another emotion went through her.

Instantly she suppressed it. No, it was just a coincidence, that was all.

It had to be.

For a moment longer she just went on staring at him, as he stared back at her, that look of appalled disbelief still in his face. Something about it finally got to her, penetrating her own complete shock at what on earth a man so bizarrely inappropriate for the rain-swept West Country was doing in front of her house.

She felt her expression stiffen.

'Yes,' she said brusquely. 'I am Laura Stowe. And you are—?'

She waited pointedly, but the man simply went on gazing at her, not bothering to veil the expression in his eyes. It was more than just surprise.

It was a look she had long been familiar with. She'd been getting it from men all her life. The look that told her, as if it had been written in letters six feet high, that so far as they were concerned she simply didn't count as a woman.

She never had.

Her grandparents, she knew, had been relieved. What they had feared most was a repeat of the fate that had overcome their beloved daughter, born so late in their lives, cherished so closely.

Until her one rash venture abroad had ruined her life.

Her grandparents had never overcome the shame of their daughter being an unmarried mother, nor the stigma of their granddaughter's illegitimacy. Despite their love for her—the more so after her mother had died—Laura knew her grandparents had never come to terms with it. It had never been mentioned, but it had been there all the time, like a stain on her skin. An embarrassment to be coped with, endured—and hidden.

Wharton was a good place to hide from the world. Remote, secluded, hard to find. But now she felt unease snake through her. Someone had found it. Someone whose apparent nationality was the most unwelcome she could think of.

But surely, *surely* that was just a coincidence?

Laura stood, staring at the man who was a million miles out of place here. The familiar look she was so used to seemed more pronounced in his dark eyes—but why wouldn't it be? she thought. A man that ludicrously handsome would never surround himself with any females who weren't his absolute equal in looks.

The beautiful people.

The old phrase formed in her mind, suiting itself totally to the man standing on her porch. The beautiful people—glamorous, rich, moving in rich, glamorous circles, in a glittering, fashionable world. A world as far away from hers as Mars.

But this wasn't Mars, this was Wharton, and it was her home, and Laura was determined to find out what this man was doing here.

She stepped forward under the porch, pushing her hood back.

'Perhaps you didn't hear me. I'm Laura Stowe. What was it you wanted?' she repeated. Her voice was clipped.

The eyes flicked over her again. The same reaction in them, but now with something more—something that didn't have to do with her appearance. Unease tensed her spine again. What was going on? Who was this man and why was he here?

Tension made her speak again. More brusquely than was polite, but that was the way it came out.

'If you can't state your business, I must ask you to leave.'

She saw the dark eyes flash—he didn't care for being spoken to in that way. Well, it was too bad. He'd turned up here out of the blue, asking for her, and now, when she'd answered him, he wasn't saying anything.

The sculpted lips tightened.

'I have a matter of significance to impart to you,' he said shortly. 'Perhaps you would do me the courtesy of opening the door so that I may talk to you indoors?'

Her hesitation was visible. A sardonic look showed in his dark eyes.

'You will be quite safe, *signorina*,' he said.

Dull colour mounted in Laura's cheeks at his words. She didn't need smart jibes to tell her she was safe from any untoward advances by men.

'This door is locked,' she told him. 'Wait here.'

Allesandro watched her turn and stomp off along the weed-strewn drive, towards the corner of the house, before disappearing out of sight. For a moment he just stared after where she had gone.

Dio, the girl was a fright! How the hell had Stefano produced offspring so dire? He'd been a good-looking man himself, and he'd hardly have bothered to seduce this girl's mother if she hadn't been pretty—so where had all that genetic legacy disappeared to? As for her personality, it matched her appearance. Ungracious and unmannerly.

He turned back to stare at the still obdurately closed and locked front door. A flurry of raindrops blew in on him, and another heavy drop landed on his shoulder from one of the several leaks in the roof. He felt his mood worsen even more.

After what seemed an interminable amount of time the door finally creaked open, and Allesandro stepped inside.

Immediately, the smell of damp assailed him. For a moment he could see nothing, then he made out a dim hallway, with a dark, cold flagstone floor, and an old chest set against the wall and a grandfather clock. The door closed behind him, cutting out some of the damp and cold, but not a great deal.

'This way,' said the female he had come a thousand miles to find.

She was still wearing those unspeakable corduroy trousers, and the absence of the hooded jacket had not improved her appearance, as her top now consisted of a baggy hand knitted jumper with a hole in one elbow and overlong sleeves. Her hair, he noted without surprise, was atrocious: a lank mop that was roughly tied back with a piece of elastic.

She took him through a baize door and into an old-fashioned kitchen, warmed, he noted thankfully, by an ancient range.

'So, who are you, and what is it that you want to tell me?' demanded the girl.

Allesandro did not answer immediately. Instead he sat himself down in the chair she had pulled out and surveyed her.

'You are Laura Stowe, you say?' he began.

The hostile look came his way again.

'As I have previously said, yes, I *am* Laura Stowe. And you are—?' she said pointedly.

Allesandro let his eyes rest on her a moment, taking in the full extent of her unprepossessingness. The girl wasn't just plain—she was ugly. Unkind it might be, but there was no other word for her appearance. She had a square face, eyes that were marred by unsightly thick brows, and a sour expression. Stefano's genes had definitely passed her by.

'I am Allesandro di Vincenzo,' he informed her, his Italian accent becoming pronounced as he said his own name. 'And I am here on behalf of Signor Viale.'

The announcement of his own name had done nothing to her blank expression, but when he said the name of her grandfather something happened to it. If he had thought she'd looked hostile before, it was as nothing to the grim, hard look that seized her expression now.

'You know of him?' Allesandro's eyebrows rose inquisitorially.

'I know the name Viale all right,' came the terse reply. 'Why are you here?' she again demanded.

Allesandro had no idea how much the girl knew about her background, so he continued. 'Signor Viale has only just learnt of your existence,' he informed her reprovingly.

For a moment emotion worked in the girl's face. Then she gave vent to it.

'That's a *lie*!' she said venomously. 'My father's always known about me!'

Allesandro's brows drew together forbiddingly. 'I am not referring to your father. I am speaking of your grandfather. Your existence has only just come to light to him.'

There was no change in her expression.

'Well, bully for him! And if that's all you've come to tell me, then you can be on your way!'

Allesandro felt his features stiffen.

'On the contrary. I am here to inform you that your grandfather, Tomaso Viale, wishes you to come to Italy.'

Now her expression changed.

'Wishes me to come to Italy?' she echoed. 'Is he mad?'

Allesandro's mouth thinned and he tamped down his rising temper at the girl's attitude.

'Miss Stowe, your grandfather is an old, frail man. The death of his son has hit him hard, and he—'

There was a rough gasp from the girl.

'My father is dead?' Her voice was blank with shock. For a moment Allesandro felt he had been too blunt, but the girl was so aggressive he didn't care. 'Stefano was killed in a power-boat crash last summer,' he said matter-of-factly.

'Last summer...' The echo of his words trailed from her. 'He's been dead all that time...'

Something seemed to shift in her eyes. Then, abruptly, the same resentful expression resumed.

'You've had a wasted journey, Signor di Vincenzo. So you might as well leave now.'

'That is not possible.' Allesandro had not raised his voice in any way, but there was an implacable note in it. 'Your grandfather wishes me to escort you to Italy.'

'I'm not going.' The flash came again in the unlovely eyes. 'My father treated my mother unforgivably. I want nothing to do with his family!'

She had spoken with a low, grim vehemence that was at one with her unappealing appearance. It irritated Allesandro. He had no wish to be here, none whatsoever, and now, for his pains, this fright of a girl was trying to send him off with a flea in his ear.

He sat back in the chair. It was time to cut to the chase.

'Perhaps you do not realise,' he said, and his dark eyes rested unreadably on his target, 'that your grandfather is a very wealthy man. One of the richest in Italy. It would be, Miss Stowe, to your clear material advantage to accede to his wishes.'

For answer she leant forward slightly, her hands touching the top of the table across from him.

'I hope he *chokes* on his wealth!' she bit out. 'Just go! Right now! Tell him, since you're his messenger boy, that so far as I'm concerned I have no grandfather! Just like his son had no daughter!'

Anger seared in Allesandro's face.

'Tomaso was not responsible for your father's refusal to acknowledge you!'

'Well, he clearly did a lousy job of bringing up his son! That was something he *did* have responsibility for, and he failed miserably! His son was despicable—so why should I have the slightest time for a man who brought up his son to be like that?'

Allesandro got to his feet. The sudden movement made the chair legs scrape on the flagstoned floor.

'*Basta!*' More Italian broke from him, sounding vehement. Then he cut back to English. 'It is as well that you are refusing to visit your grandfather. You would be a great disappointment to him. As it is,' he said cuttingly, 'I am now facing the task of telling an old, sick man, mourning the tragic death of his only son, that his last remaining relative on earth is an ill-mannered, inconsiderate, self-righteous female prepared to condemn him sight unseen. I'll take my leave of you.'

Without another word he strode out of the room, back down the corridor to the front door. She heard the front door thump shut, and then the sound of an engine starting, of a car moving off, soon dying away.

She was, she realised, shaking very slightly.

Aftershock, she thought. Out of nowhere, for the first time in her life, contact had been made by her father's family in Italy. All her life his name had been excoriated, all mention of him—and they had been few and far between—prefixed by condemnation and unforgiving hostility. She had grown up from infancy with her mother dead, and her grandparents making it extremely plain to her just how despicable her father had been.

But now he's dead...

A stab of pain went through her again. She had never expected—let alone wanted—to see him, or meet him, or know anything more about him. Yet to have been told so bluntly that he was dead had still been a shock. For a second so brief it was extinguished almost as soon as it occurred, a sense of grief went through her.

My father is dead. I never knew him, and now I never will...

Then she rallied. She knew enough about him to know that he would not have been worth knowing.

He rejected you. Rejected you so entirely that he completely and absolutely ignored your existence. He didn't give a damn about you...

He was nothing but a spoilt, self-indulgent playboy, who used women like playthings. Getting away with it because he was rich and handsome.

Like the man who was sent here.

Unwillingly, her eyes flicked to where he had been sitting, and her expression soured even more. Then she straightened her shoulders. There was work to be done, and she had better get on with it. Grim-faced, she plodded back out into the yard, and set off to gather another load of kindling in the rain.

Allesandro sank into the soft chintz-covered armchair with a sense of relief and looked around the warm, elegant drawing room of the Lidford House Hotel, which his PA had booked for an overnight stay before flying back to Rome. Now *this* was the way a country house in England should be—not like Laura Stowe's decaying ruin.

He took a sip of martini, savouring its dry tang as if it were washing a bad taste out of his mouth. *Dio*, but the girl was a termagant! Without a redeeming feature—in appearance or personality—to her name. Though he had resented Tomaso's manipulation of him, now he could only pity the man for his granddaughter. He wouldn't wish her on anyone! Allesandro's face shadowed momentarily. Tomaso's disappointment would be acute. It did not take much to realise that what he had been hoping for was not just comfort in his bereavement but also, eventually, a hope of his own progeny.

Well, he could whistle for a husband for the girl—that much was plain. As plain as she herself was.

He took another sip of his martini, enjoying the warmth from the roaring fire in front of him.

In other circumstances he would have pitied the girl for her complete lack of looks. But her manners and personality had been so abrasive, so unpleasant, that they put her beyond pity.

Impatiently he reached for the leatherbound menu to decide what to have for dinner. Tomaso's unlovely granddaughter was no longer his concern. He had done what Tomaso had asked, and if she were refusing to come to Italy, so be it.

It was not his problem.

Except when Allesandro returned to Italy, he discovered that Tomaso did not see it that way.

'He's done *what*?' Two days later, Allesandro's voice was rigid with disbelief.

But the question was rhetorical. The answer to it was in front of his eyes, in the tersely worded memo that his PA had silently handed him. Signed by the chairman of Viale-Vincenzo, informing him that his services as chief executive would no longer be required.

A rage such as he had never known permeated through Allesandro. He might still be a major shareholder in Viale-Vincenzo, but now he would no longer even have day-to-day control of the company, let alone the long-term control that the chairmanship would have given him. He knew exactly what was behind this. Tomaso had not accepted Laura Stowe's refusal to visit him. Allesandro had balked at spelling out just how hostile the girl had been to him. Now he wished he'd been less sensitive of Tomaso's feelings.

'Get me Tomaso on the phone,' he ordered savagely. 'Now!'

CHAPTER TWO

LAURA picked up the post that had fallen through the letterbox, her expression bleak. Yesterday's post had brought grim news. A final reminder from the taxman warned her that late payment would incur interest charges, and a letter from the auction house had valued the remaining antiques at considerably less than the sum the taxman required.

Despair and fear were gnawing at her. Day by day she was edging closer to the bleak prospect of having to sell Wharton. Her heart clawed at the thought.

I can't sell! I just can't! There has to be something—something I can do to keep it going!

If she could just pay the taxman, she would have a chance. She could raise a mortgage on the property and then use the money to convert the house into a holiday let, as planned. The lettings would then pay the mortgage and maintenance costs. But if she couldn't pay the tax...

Desperation knifed through her again.

As she continued to consider her bleak future, her hands stilled suddenly on one of the letters. It was a thick white envelope, and the stamp was Italian. Grimly she ripped it open. Inside were three things: a letter, an airline ticket...

And a cheque.

A cheque drawn on Viale-Vincenzo. In a sum that brought a rasp to her throat.

Slowly she looked at the letter, written on company paper. It was not informative, merely drew her attention to the enclosed cheque and ticket. As she flicked open the ticket she saw it was from Heathrow to Rome, and was dated for a week's time. It was also executive class. Attached to the back of the letter was a second page of closely printed Italian that she could not understand. Obviously this document must explain that the cheque was a gift in return for her visiting her grandfather in Italy.

Carefully, Laura replaced everything inside the envelope, and went to sit down at the kitchen table. She stared at the envelope in front of her, so different from yesterday's communication from the Inland Revenue and the auctioneer.

Suddenly temptation, like an overpowering wave, swept through her.

I'll pay the cheque back—every last penny, with interest!— once I've got the mortgage through. But the taxman won't wait— I've got to settle that first, in any way I can!

But not this way, she riposted mentally. She couldn't touch a penny of Viale money! Her grandfather would turn in his grave if she did—especially after the way Stefano Viale had treated his daughter..

But surely the Viale family owed him, too?

They owe you—and your mother, and your grandparents— for all the years of struggle, because of what your father did. They owe you...

Not a penny in child maintenance had her mother received. It had been Laura's grandparents who had kept her and her mother, who had brought her up, paid for her education and keep, shod and housed her. Stefano Viale—whose father, according to the handsome lordly gofer who had told her, was one of the richest men in Italy—had not parted with a penny of his money.

The cheque's just back-payment. That's all!

But if she did take the cheque, she would have to do what it was bribing her to do. Her stomach hollowed. She would have to go to Italy and face her father's family.

Her face hardened. She had to save Wharton. It was her home, her haven! She had always lived here, helping to take the burden of its upkeep off her increasingly frail grandparents. She couldn't lose it now! She just couldn't! She stared blankly at the cheque in her hand, stomach churning.

I'm going to have to do it. I'm going to have to go to Italy. I don't want to—I don't want to so badly that it hurts. But if I want that money—money I need to help save Wharton—then I'm going to have to do it.

Laura stared out of the porthole over the fleecy white clouds, her expression tight. With every atom of her body she wished to heaven she was not here. But it was too late now. She was on her way, and there was nothing she could do about it.

'Champagne?' The flight attendant, a tray of foaming glasses in her hand, was smiling down at her, as if she didn't look totally out of place in an executive class seat.

'Thank you,' said Laura awkwardly, taking a glass. Well, why not? she thought defiantly. After all, she had something to drink to.

She lifted her glass a fraction.

'To Wharton,' she whispered. 'To my home. And *damn* my father's family!'

A man was holding up a sign with her name on it as she walked out into the arrivals section at Fiumicino airport. Landing in Rome had been strange. She had seldom been abroad. There had been a school trip to Brussels, and her grandparents had once taken her to the Netherlands. But Italy, of course, had been out for obvious reasons.

And she didn't want to be here now. Resentment, resistance, and a horrible churning emotion she could not name sat heavily on her as she clumped after the man holding the sign, who was now carrying her single piece of luggage. Outdoors, the difference in temperature from still-wintry Devon struck her. It was not warm, but it was definitely mild. Thin sunshine brightened the air, but it could not brighten her mood. The ordeal ahead of her suddenly seemed very real. She clenched her jaw and climbed into the back of the smart black saloon that had been sent for her.

It was only as she sank into the deep, soft leather of her seat that she realised she was not alone in the car.

Allesandro di Vincenzo sat beside her. His dark eyes surveyed her critically.

'So,' he said, 'you finally came. I thought the fat cheque I paid you might change your mind.'

His voice was caustic, as was the look he gave her.

The intervening time since his rain-sodden descent on Laura Stowe had not improved her looks, observed Allesandro critically. She looked every bit as much of a fright now as she had then. Oh, she'd clearly made some degree of effort to look less bedraggled than before, but to hopeless effect. Although she was no longer wearing those unspeakable corduroy trousers and that thick unravelled jumper, her skirt was ill-fitting, clearly cheap, and her blouse bagged around her bust and waist. She wore thick stockings and heavy-soled flat shoes. Her hair was unkempt, completely unstyled, and still tied back with an elasticated band in a clump at the back of her neck. Her eyebrows still beetled across her brow, and she wore no make-up whatsoever. As his gaze narrowed, he knew why. Because it wouldn't do anything for her.

Nothing could—that much was obvious.

His mouth tightened. Tomaso was welcome to her. After this second round of even more base manipulation, Allesandro's sympathy for Tomaso was at rock-bottom—even allowing for the old man's emotional state. He would deliver the girl and get back to his life—running Viale-Vincenzo, at least as CEO again, even though Tomaso was still holding out on the chairmanship. If the old man reneged on that again, now that he'd actually delivered the damn girl to him... He snapped his mind away and opened his laptop, immediately burying himself in work and ignoring the other passenger in the car.

Laura spent the journey staring out of the window. They seemed to be heading deep into the Italian countryside, rather than heading into Rome. But wherever her grandfather was, she didn't want to meet him.

She also didn't want to be in a car with Allesandro di Vincenzo. It had been an unpleasant surprise to see him again. A discomforting one. She'd always done her best in life to avoid the company of men, removing herself before they did. A man who was as ridiculously good-looking as Allesandro di Vincenzo, with all his expensive glamour and effortless sex appeal, simply made her even more acutely uncomfortable. Even without all the business about her father and his family, it was totally obvious that a man like that would endure her company only under duress.

A shuttered look showed in her face. She'd read somewhere that beautiful women and handsome men tended to be nicer than those not so beautiful or handsome. The reason, the article had explained, was that the beautiful people had always been feted and welcomed and admired, and so naturally they found the world a good place to live in. Plain people, like herself, were far less sure of a welcome by others. It made them awkward and self-conscious, uncertain.

Well, that was true of her, she thought, staring up through the windscreen. She'd felt an outsider all her life, thanks mainly to the circumstances of her birth. But then adolescence had arrived, bringing home to her the tough truth about her appearance, and that sense of being an outsider—shut out from the normal activities of her age group—had been exacerbated a thousand times.

Laura had finally realised that she had two choices in life. Either to be bitter about being so unattractive, or to get over it and move on. There were other things in life that were worthwhile, and if she just totally ignored her own appearance then she wouldn't be bothered by it.

And now she refused to be troubled by it. She wore clothes she could afford, which were serviceable and comfortable. She didn't bother about her hair—never spending money getting it cut, just tying it back out of the way. And as for make-up, she'd save her money for something more useful. Like groceries and bills.

And what did she care about a man like Allesandro di Vincenzo, as alien to her as if he'd come from another planet, looking at her with disdain? It was a lot easier when he was doing what he was doing now—completely ignoring her. Immersed in his laptop, he tapped away at the keyboard.

He must, she realised, be a key part of Viale-Vincenzo. He was clearly rich, and there was an aura of command about him even though he must only be in his early thirties, she surmised.

She gave a private sour smile as she gazed out of the window, then deliberately forced her mind away from the man in the car. Instead, she looked at the passing countryside as the car sped smoothly along the *autostrada*.

This was Italy—the cypresses, the olive groves, the fields and the hills, the vineyards and the red-tiled houses. All bathed in sunlight.

This is my country, as much as England is.

Something stirred inside her, but she crushed it down. She might be half-Italian, but it was by accident only, not intent. Her upbringing was English—all English. This was an alien place. She did not belong here. It meant nothing to her. Nothing at all.

Deliberately, she started to run through all the repairs that needed doing at Wharton. That was the only place that meant anything to her.

Not anything here.

Laura got out of the car and looked around her. Involuntarily, her eyes widened. The house in front of her was huge. A grand, aristocratic villa, no less, made of cream-coloured stone. Sash windows marched along the frontage, winking in the sunlight and on the other side of the gravelled drive on which the car had drawn up formal gardens stretched away down a gentle slope. Even at this time of year she could see the grounds were perfectly manicured.

Tension knotted inside her like a ball of steel wool.

She was here, in Italy. Inside this vast house was her only living relative. The father of the man who had fathered her. Father of the man who had destroyed her mother with his callousness and cruelty, and who had refused to acknowledge his own daughter's existence.

She wanted to run. Bolt. Get away as fast and as far as she could. She wanted to go home, *be* home—the only home she had ever known, the only home she wanted. She wanted nothing, *nothing* of what was here.

She stared about her. That strange pang came again, very deep within. If the man who had fathered her hadn't been the complete bastard that he had, she might have known this place. Might have been brought here for holidays. Might have run laughing through the gardens as a child. Her mother might have been here too—alive and happy with the man she loved...

But Stefano Viale had not been interested in love, or marriage, or his own daughter. He had made that very, very plain.

Inside her head, she heard again her grandmother's stricken voice.

'He never wrote, not once. Never answered any of your mother's letters. She was heartbroken—just heartbroken. Not a single letter, not a single kind word to her. He'd taken her innocence, used her and thrown her away!'

Laura's expression hardened. That had been the reality she had grown up with.

Father? She didn't have one. She never had.

And she didn't have a grandfather either. Whatever the man waiting for her inside wanted to call himself.

'This way.'

The terse, impersonal tones of Allesandro di Vincenzo interrupted her baleful thoughts. She was being directed indoors, and with an increasing sense of oppression she walked inside into a vast marble-floored entrance hall.

Allesandro strode past her, towards a pair of double doors beyond. He threw them open and walked in. Tomaso was there, at his desk by the window. He looked up immediately. There was a taut expression on his face. Tense. Expectant.

Suddenly, for all that the old man had manipulated him

shamelessly, Allesandro felt he could not do this to him. He should go in first, warn the old man what he was about to get by way of a granddaughter. Then he crushed his compunction. Tomaso was playing hardball—deliberately using Allesandro's desire for control of Viale-Vincenzo in order to make him do what he wanted. And if what he wanted was his deeply unpleasant granddaughter, he could have her.

Behind him Allesandro could hear the heavy plod of unfeminine feet shod in flat clumpy shoes that no Italian woman this side of a lunatic asylum would even have possessed, let alone worn.

The old man was getting to his feet.

'Tomaso—your granddaughter,' announced Allesandro, his voice studiously expressionless. 'Laura Stowe.'

But Tomaso was not looking at him. He was staring past the younger man to the female figure that had walked in behind him. Allesandro watched his face as the old man's expression changed.

It became bland, unreadable.

'Laura—' said Tomaso, and held his hand towards her.

The girl was standing there, ignoring the hand that stretched out to her. Her face was shuttered, the way it had been the entire journey. The lack of expression made the girl look like a pudding—one of those stodgy English ones, with suet in them.

'I am your grandfather,' said Tomaso. The face might be bland, Allesandro thought, eyes narrowing minutely, but the voice was not. It was audibly suppressing emotion.

Something flickered angrily in the girl's face.

'My grandfather is dead. You are merely the father of the man who ruined my mother's life.'

The aggression in her tone was unequivocal. For a moment Allesandro saw new emotion in Tomaso's face. Shock. Naked and raw.

The girl held her pitiless gaze.

'The only reason I'm here,' she told him, 'is because that man—' she nodded curtly in Allesandro's direction, and he felt a spurt of vicious anger both at her manner, and at what he knew was coming next '—bribed me to come.'

'He *bribed* you?' The old man's voice was a disbelieving echo.

'Yes.' Allesandro watched, aghast, as the girl spoke bluntly. 'I don't want anything to do with you, or anyone connected with the man who treated my mother so unforgivably! I can't imagine why you thought I would have the slightest desire or interest in meeting you—any more than the man who fathered me had the slightest desire or interest in my existence, or in what he'd done to my mother!' A sharp, tight breath made her pause, and then she went on. 'I'm sorry your son is dead—but it's nothing to do with me. Nothing. Because your son wasn't anything to do with me. He made that totally clear even before I was born!'

Shock edged Tomaso's face. 'This is not how I— This is not—' He faltered. He looked across at the girl, half turned away. 'I thought—I thought you would be glad—glad that I had sought you out...'

His face greyed, and then suddenly his hand was clutching at his heart. Allesandro started forward, catching him as he fell.

The next hour was endless. Allesandro had immediately summoned an ambulance, and Tomaso had been rushed to hospital. To Allesandro's relief he was soon pronounced out of danger, even though he was being kept in overnight for monitoring.

Whatever kind of seizure Tomaso had had, Allesandro knew only one thing. That harpy, with her venomous tirade, had been responsible. His eyes darkened now, as he glared at the girl sitting stony-faced in the car taking them back to Tomaso's villa. Her hands were clenched in her lap. She'd sat just like that in the hospital lobby while Allesandro had accompanied Tomaso into the ward.

'Is he going to be all right?' she asked suddenly.

'You *care*?' Allesandro derided.

'I told you—I'm sorry his son is dead, and I'm sorry he collapsed. I wouldn't want him to die. I wouldn't want anyone to die.' Her voice was terse and jerky.

'Big of you,' he replied. 'But if you really want to be big, you'd better do what he wants and stay at the villa until he's well enough to see you. God knows why he should want to, but he said he did before I left him.'

He got no answer from her, only a shoulder turning away from him, maximising the distance between them. The movement irritated him. If there was a female in the world less likely to engage his interest, she was beyond imagining.

CHAPTER THREE

LAURA sat on the bed in the bedroom she'd been shown to by one of the household staff, and stared out of the window. The view was beautiful. Formal Italianate gardens, just like in a guidebook, and then a vista of olive groves, narrow dark cypresses and rolling hills.

She turned away. She didn't want to see it. Didn't want to be here. Didn't want to be in Italy, in her grandfather's villa—

He's not your grandfather—don't think of him that way!

Genes didn't make you family. She had half her father's genes, but that didn't make her his daughter. It certainly hadn't in his eyes, anyway.

She lay back on the bed. She was tired. She'd had to catch an early bus to Exeter, then the coach to Heathrow, then the flight here. Her eyelids grew heavy...

She must have nodded off, because the next thing she knew there was a maid in the room, informing her that dinner was served. Reluctantly Laura went downstairs, prudently taking a book with her. She'd have rather eaten in her room, but didn't want to be a nuisance.

A manservant waiting at the foot of the sweeping stairs conducted her to a room opening off the hall. She walked in, and stopped dead.

Allesandro di Vincenzo was there, already seated at the table. As she clomped in he got to his feet. There was a sheaf of papers beside his place, and he'd obviously been reading them.

'I thought you'd gone,' she blurted, before she could stop herself.

'Alas, no,' came his reply. It was smooth, but terse. And very unfriendly. 'Much though I would have preferred to return to Rome, I would not dream of abandoning a hospitalised Tomaso to nothing more than *your* loving presence.'

Laura felt colour mottle her cheeks.

'How is he?' she asked, as she went and took the only other place laid at the vast table—directly opposite Allesandro. It made him seem closer than she wanted him to be. But then she didn't want him anywhere near her at all anyway.

The feeling was doubtless mutual, she realised, intercepting a black look from him as she pulled in her chair.

'His condition is stable,' he said. 'As if you care.'

Her colour mounted. 'I don't want him to die—I told you that.'

'And as I told you—that's big of you,' Allesandro returned. He frowned. 'Do you have nothing better to wear for dinner?' he demanded, his eyes flicking dismissively over her clothes.

'No,' said Laura. If she'd known he was going to be here she'd have insisted on a meal in her room. He was the last person she wanted to spend time with. She opened her book and started to read. To her relief, her unwelcome dining partner returned his attention to his papers.

The meal that followed was ludicrously formal, to Laura's mind. There were too many courses, and it went on for ages. The only compensation—for the company was even worse than the formality and the length of the meal—was the food, which was incredibly delicious. As she scraped up the last of the delicious sauce accompanying the beautifully cooked lamb, Laura realised she was under surveillance.

'Do you always eat so much?'

Laura stared blankly. She liked food. She always had. Comfort eating, the magazine articles called it, but she didn't care. Her lifestyle was not sedentary, and with all the sheer physical slog of looking after Wharton, plus the long, solitary walks she loved to take through the countryside, she had a good appetite.

'Sturdy' her grandmother had always called her. Probably she would run to fat when she was middle aged—as her grandmother had.

Now, she swallowed the last mouthful, put her cutlery back on the plate, and said baldly, 'Yes.'

Then she went on reading.

Allesandro glowered from his seat across the table. None of the women he knew could put food away like that. Even though it was impossible to see her figure in those shapeless clothes, if she were eating like that she could hardly be anything but overweight. He went back to his report on market conditions in South America. Laura Stowe could be the size of an elephant for all he cared.

The following day the hospital phoned to say that Tomaso was up to receiving visitors. Relieved, Allesandro marshalled Laura into the waiting car. As she sat, her hands twisting uneasily in her lap, he suddenly asked, 'What is wrong with your hands?'

She glanced down. 'Nothing. Why?'

He hadn't noticed them before. But then, it was hard to when there was the rest of her unappealing appearance to attempt to ignore.

'They are covered in scratches,' he said.

She shrugged. 'They're healing. I was clearing some brambles in the garden the day before I came out here.' She turned her hands over. The palms were just as scratched, plus rough and callused.

'What do you *do* to yourself?' he demanded.

She looked at him expressionlessly. 'I work. Wharton doesn't look after itself.'

His face tightened. 'You have staff, surely?'

She rolled her eyes. 'Oh, yes—four housemaids and just as many gardeners!'

He took a breath. 'Well, perhaps now, with the money I paid you, you can afford to hire some help.'

'I doubt the Inland Revenue will see it that way,' she said dryly.

'*Como?*' Allesandro's eyebrows drew together.

'Your cheque paid off the first tranche of death duties I owe. That's why I accepted it. I'd have torn it to shreds otherwise. But…' she shrugged, looking at him defiantly '…I'm going to fight tooth and nail to keep Wharton. And you'll get your money back, Signor di Vincenzo. I assure you. When I'm finally earning money from holiday lets at Wharton—'

'You think someone will *pay* to stay there?' Allesandro interjected incredulously. 'It's a rain-sodden, decaying wreck!'

Her chin lifted. 'I'll renovate it,' she said. 'I won't sell up unless I'm absolutely forced to!'

Allesandro was looking at her strangely.

'You are *attached* to the place?' He made it sound as though she enjoyed eating rotten meat.

'It's my home,' she said tightly.

He gestured with his hand around him. 'But you have a new home here, for the asking,' he said.

Her expression tightened even more.

'And also,' he went on, with the same strange look in his face, 'you now need have no more money worries. Your grandfather will lavish on you whatever you want.'

A hard light entered her eyes. 'What a pity the man he fathered didn't think to lavish the one thing on his daughter that she actually would have valued—his acknowledgement of her existence!'

Allesandro's expression changed. 'Stefano was a—a law unto himself. He did what he wanted. He was—'

'A bastard,' said Laura. 'Like me.'

Her jaw was set. She looked belligerent.

Cussed. Sullen. Ill-tempered.

The familiar adjectives scrolled in Allesandro's mind. Then another one entered. Where it had come from, he had no idea. But suddenly it was there all the same.

Bleak, with an empty look in her eyes.

He thrust it aside. Laura Stowe wasn't someone he wanted to feel sorry for.

At the hospital his instructions were terse.

'Say anything to upset Tomaso and you will be sorry, I promise you.'

Laura only looked away. The last time she'd been in a hospital ward it had been to see her grandfather, the day he had finally died of heart failure, mere months after her grandmother's death. As she followed Allesandro into the intensive care room, and saw the solitary figure surrounded by instruments and electronics, his body wired up to them and a drip in his arm, she swallowed hard.

The figure in the bed was so frail. As frail as her grandfather had been.

But this is my grandfather. The thought pierced her suddenly.

She shook her head. No—no, it *wasn't*! She wouldn't let him be. She wouldn't let anything of this touch her. She would block it out of her mind, her life, her existence.

This is nothing to do with me! Nothing!

But as she walked in, the head lying on the white pillow turned towards her.

'Laura—'

The voice was thin, but it had lifted on her name.

Silently, with clear effort, a frail hand was held out to her.

'You came,' he said. Dark eyes rested on her. In them Laura thought she saw something she had not expected to see.

Gratitude.

She walked forward. She didn't take the hand, and Tomaso let it fall back on the bed. A little of the light went out of his eyes. It made Laura feel bad, but she did not want to touch him.

'How—how are you?' she said, her voice stiff and awkward.

There was a flicker in the dark eyes. 'Better for seeing you. Thank you—thank you for staying. For allowing me—'

He took a breath. It sounded difficult and rasping.

'Please, won't you sit down?'

Heavily, she sank down into the chair by the bed. Tomaso's gaze went past her to the figure standing in the doorway.

'I'm staying,' said Allesandro in Italian. 'I don't want her upsetting you.'

Tomaso's expression changed. 'I think I will be safe enough. Thank you for bringing her to me, Allesandro, but now—'

Reluctantly, Allesandro left. The heart monitor would give the alarm if the crash team were to be needed precipitately. Moodily, he went on pacing up and down the corridor.

Inside the intensive care room, Tomaso's gaze returned to Laura. She bit her lip. Tension wracked her body. Her throat was as tight as a drum.

'Laura—my child. I have something I must say to you. I ask you, most humbly, to allow me to say it.' The rasp in his voice came again. 'Then, if you still wish, leave and return to England. With my blessing. Should you want it,' he added, and there was a wry ruefulness in his voice.

He paused a moment, as if he were gathering strength. From the corner of her eye Laura could see the oscilloscope pulse to the beating of his heart. Her own heart seemed to be thudding heavily inside her.

She wanted to go. Wanted to bolt, run, get out of here. March away on heavy, hard feet. March all the way back to England. To Wharton. Shut herself in the house and never come out. Never. But she couldn't. She couldn't bring herself to do it. Something kept her glued to the chair. It was probably tension. Nerves. What else could it be?

She felt Tomaso's gaze on her—as if, she realised, he was steeling himself to say something more. As if he was wary of her reaction. Anxious, even. Then, with that weak rasp still in his voice, he spoke. His eyes rested on her, and his head turned towards her.

'Lying here has given me time to think. To remember. And I have thought much and remembered much. I have remembered Stefano. Not as I last saw him—not as he was in those last years of his life—but long ago. When he was your age. Younger. Even younger.'

He took a breath, then went on. 'But I don't have very many memories of him. Nor as a boy. You see…' his eyes wavered a moment '…I did not spend a great deal of time with him. I was busy making money. Stefano I left to his mother. She doted on him.' His gaze wavered again. 'I was too busy to spend much time with her, either. So she lavished on him all the devotion and attention that I was too busy to accept from her. Stefano was always wild, obsessed with his power boats.'

He was silent a moment, whether to gather his strength or to dwell on his dead son Laura didn't know. She only knew that she was stretched tight, like a pulled wire. She wanted Tomaso not to have spoken. Not to have drawn an image of a boy, a young man, half-neglected, half-spoilt, taking what he wanted and ignoring the consequences.

And that included my mother! He took her and dumped her! And be damned to the consequences—including getting her pregnant!

Anger, familiar like an old hair shirt, rubbed against her.

Tomaso was speaking again. His voice had changed now.

'A man wishes to be proud of his son. But how can I be proud that my son seduced and abandoned the mother of his child? Ignored her existence—and yours.' The eyes rested on her, and she could see pain in them. And remorse.

'It was crass of me. Stupid, insensitive—and selfish—of me to think you could have any wish to know your father's family,' he said heavily. 'All your life you have lived knowing what my son did to your mother, and to you. And for me to think that in an instant everything could be forgiven and forgotten was stupid of me in the extreme. There is anger in you—a lifetime of anger—and I cannot ignore that. I must not.'

He took another breath. His eyes hung on hers.

'Go home, if you wish. I have no right to you at all. None. I have been foolish and greedy. I wanted to do well by you, but I cannot wash away the past. I cannot undo what Stefano did to you, to your mother, and to her parents. I have not been a good father, Laura. I wished to make up for that by being a good grandfather to you, but…'

His voice trailed off.

Laura went on sitting there. She could hear small sounds—

the click of an electrical unit, the sound of a bird, a car, some muffled voices in the corridor outside.

It was very quiet.

Then, suddenly, it burst from her.

'How could he do it? *How?* How could he just ignore her like that? It wasn't as if he even wrote back to say he didn't believe the baby was his! He just totally ignored her! She wrote and wrote, and he never, *ever* got back in touch. She was just a nuisance! That's all she was to him! And so was I. He didn't even want to know.'

There was a horrible cracking noise in her throat.

'He didn't want me,' she said.

Two spots of colour were burning in her cheeks. They did not flatter her. She got to her feet. It was an abrupt, jerky movement. She turned away, towards the door, taking a sharp, agonising breath. She took a step forward, not looking at the man who stood in the doorway. Not looking at anyone or anything.

'But *I* want you, Laura.'

Her head whipped round.

Tomaso had reached out his hand again.

'*I* want you,' he said again. There was an impulse in his voice, an urgency. 'It is too late for Stefano, but I ask—I ask if it will not be too late for me. You are my only kin. All I have. Give me a little, just a little of your time. I shall not ask for much. Only the chance, poor as it is, to pass a little time with you.'

His eyes were holding hers, as if they were cast upon a lifeline. Slowly, very slowly, not sure what she was doing, let alone why, or whether she should turn, and walk on heavy, rapid feet, as far away as possible, Laura reached out and touched the tips of his fingers held out towards her. Then she dropped her arm to her side.

'Thank you,' said Tomaso quietly.

Laura was silent on the way back to the villa, staring out of the car window. Allesandro let his gaze rest on her from time to time. She'd closed herself up, like a clam. But there was something different about her. Something…softer.

He frowned. Could that really be true? Surely not. It was an absurd word to use about Laura Stowe. She was as hard and as unyielding as granite, her manner as abrasive. Harsh and unlovely.

His eyes studied her as she stared out of the window, locked in on herself. Yes, it was there still, that change in her expression. Almost imperceptible, but there all the same.

And there was something else about her, he realised frowningly, trying to put his finger on what else had changed about her.

Then it came to him.

Somehow—he didn't know how—with that slightly, oh, so slightly softer expression—she didn't look quite so awful.

He shook the thought aside. It was nothing to do with him what she looked like—only whether she was going to make good on what she had said to Tomaso or not. He needed to know. If she were staying, then at last the way would be clear for Tomaso to make good on his promise to him and hand over the chairmanship.

'So,' he heard himself ask abruptly, 'what are you going to do now? Bolt back to England? Or give your grandfather some of your precious time?'

His voice sounded brusque in the confines of the car. Brusquer than he'd meant. Laura turned her head.

'I'll…' She swallowed. 'I'll stay for a bit. Till he's better. I suppose I don't have to go home right away.'

Any time would be too soon to go back to that rain-sodden dump, thought Allesandro, thinking unpleasurably about the wreck she lived in. What on earth did she want to keep it for? Anyway, if she made her peace with Tomaso, as she might just have done now, she wouldn't need it any more.

Just as Tomaso would not need the chairmanship of Viale-Vincenzo any more.

A spurt of impatience went through Allesandro. He wanted to be off, back to Rome. Away from all this. Preparing to take full control of the company.

Enjoying Delia Dellatore.

Deliberately, he let his thoughts conjure her image in his mind. Chic, fashionable, sensual.

His eyes flickered sideways one last time.

The contrast between the woman in his mind and the female sitting there like a sack of potatoes couldn't have been more different.

He looked away. She was nothing to do with him. And now he was done with her. The moment they were back at the villa he'd return to Rome. He slid out his mobile, phoning his PA to let her know his plans. Relief washed through him. He was getting out of here, *prontissimo*.

CHAPTER FOUR

ALLESANDRO must have left the villa at some point that afternoon, but Laura did not pay his departure any attention. Her mind was too full of other things.

What had she done? Emotion twisted inside her. She had dropped her guard against a man she had been determined to stonewall, to deny any place in her life. Her hands knotted against each other, fingers crushing.

What have I done? she thought again, agitated and unhappy, heart stormy.

But she knew. She knew in her heart of hearts what she had done. She had acknowledged Tomaso Viale as her grandfather.

And she would stay with him—just for a while. Until he was better. It wouldn't kill her to do that, would it?

When he was brought home the following day, carried in on a stretcher, she hurried out of the music room, where she had incarcerated herself, and felt again that strange pang go through her at the sight of his frail figure. As his eyes went to her, they lit at the sight of her.

'You didn't leave,' he said.

She shook her head. There was a thickness in her throat.

'No,' she managed to say. Then, 'How…how are you feeling?'

He gave a wry smile. 'The better for seeing you, my child.'

She gave an uncertain smile, and watched as he was borne aloft up the wide marble stairs.

He asked for her, later on in the day, and she went. He'd been installed in what seemed to her a palatial room, with a vast tester bed and ornate antique furniture. She personally found it very overdone, but it was obviously what he liked. She felt a strange sense of indulgence tug at her. Tomaso saw her smile to herself as she glanced around the room.

'You think it a little too much, no?' he said.

'It's the opposite of my grandfather—my...' She paused awkwardly. 'My other grandfather. He was Spartan in his tastes. He thought only foreigners went in for fancy décor.'

Tomaso looked ruefully humorous. 'Well, I am foreign, so that must account for it.' He patted the side of the huge bed he was propped up in, and without thinking Laura found herself crossing to sit on it. 'When I was a boy we were very poor. We lived in a bleak, post-war concrete apartment block in a grim suburb of Torino, with cheap utility furniture. I always promised myself the good things in life.'

He glanced around, and Laura could see the satisfaction in his face at all he had. And the pride, too.

'Did you really start from nothing?' she asked.

'Nothing but my nerve and my confidence,' he replied promptly.

He was looking better, Laura thought, his colour stronger, and he was no longer wired up, although a mobile heart monitor station stood beside the bed.

'I was determined to make money—a lot of money!—and I did!' he went on.

'My grandfather—my other one—' it was easier to say this time, she found '—never talked about money. It was one of those things that was never mentioned.'

'Ah,' said Tomaso shrewdly. 'That is always the way of those who were born to it. Never the way of those who have to make it themselves. Allesandro's father was the same—he thought profit a dirty word.' His voice edged slightly. 'But he enjoyed the money we made, all the same.'

'Why did he go into trade?' Laura asked, unconsciously curious to discover more about Allesandro's family background.

'He was broke. That was why,' Tomaso said bluntly. 'So he graciously consented to be my partner when I approached him to join forces. For me, he was very useful—he could open doors that were closed to me with all his high-society friends, especially those in banking and finance. But he was never interested in business the way I was. Now, young Allesandro...' Tomaso's voice changed suddenly. 'He is very different.'

'He seems to work all the time,' Laura said. 'His nose is always buried in his laptop or in papers.'

'He wants my job. And the company to go with it.' Tomaso's voice was even blunter now. 'He is completely different from his father. He could see how his father had little real power in the company—did not want it, did not seek it!—but Allesandro always resented that. He felt it as a slight to his father. But he also acknowledged that his father was uninterested in running the company anyway. As was Stefano.'

There was a shadow suddenly in Tomaso's eyes, and Laura felt a stab of discomfort, of raw emotion, at the mention of the man who had fathered her.

Tomaso lifted a hand, as if to dispel the shadow. 'Had Stefano lived, Allesandro would have manoeuvred to do a deal with him—take over the company in exchange for buying him out. Let him go to all his beloved lethal powerboats. Stefano would have agreed. I have no illusions about that—as I told you, he was only interested in spending money, not increasing it. But whether I would have agreed...?' He shook his head. 'Perhaps I would. For what else was to happen to the company after my death? Of course, had Stefano married—'

His voice broke off. Laura felt emotion sting inside her again. Tomaso's eyes were focussed on her. Suddenly he looked neither frail, nor ill, nor even old.

'Make no mistake, my child. Had I the slightest knowledge of what had happened so many years ago, him leaving your mother pregnant with you, he would have married her the next day. I would have seen to it.'

Laura bit her lip. She swallowed.

'Probably that's why he made sure you never found out,' she said in a low, strained voice. 'He obviously wasn't the marrying kind—not if he never married at all.'

Tomaso's voice edged again. 'No, he was a philanderer—nothing more. A playboy. He lived a wild, self-indulgent bachelor life. Many times I made it clear I expected him to marry and produce an heir for me—but he never did. Not even his mother could persuade him—not that she ever thought any woman good enough for him!'

He fell silent, his eyes shifting away from Laura.

They weren't happy, she found herself thinking. *For all their money, they weren't happy. None of them.*

His eyes came back to Laura. He looked suddenly tired, weary and old.

She stood up. 'I've tired you,' she said awkwardly. 'Your nurse said five minutes and no more.'

An imperious hand gestured away such diktat.

'She fusses because she is paid to fuss,' he said. Abruptly, he shot at her, 'How much money did Allesandro give you to come here?' Dark, penetrating eyes bored into hers.

The question had come out of nowhere, and Laura felt her face mottle. Defensively, she said, 'Enough to persuade me, evidently!'

Sharp humour glinted in Tomaso's eyes.

'Quite right—reveal nothing that you need not,' he said. There was approval in his voice. 'However much it was, Allesandro will have considered it cheap. Too much is at stake for him. His back is against the wall, and he knows it.'

Laura frowned. Allesandro di Vincenzo did not seem like a man with his back against the wall. Not unless he lounged against it with an elegance that would make females swoon by the dozen!

Tomaso enlightened her. 'I told you—he wants my job. I am chairman of Viale-Vincenzo, and it galls him. Even as chief executive he can do nothing without my consent, which frustrates him. He wants to be in sole control, and he assumes that now Stefano is dead I am the only impediment to his ambition. I set him a task, like a king in a knightly tale—his quest was to bring you to me. Now he is waiting for his reward.'

He was looking at her with a speculative expression, as if considering something. 'Tell me, Laura, do you play chess?'

'A little,' she answered.

'Good,' he said. 'We'll play after dinner.'

It was the strangest time for Laura. She felt unreal, as if the universe she had lived in for the past twenty-four years had shifted dimension. Or opened to another one.

The world of her father's family. Alien, strange. But now—day by day, little by little—increasingly less so.

It was a slow journey, and she took it slowly. Warily. Uncertainly. Awkwardly. But step by step it was a journey she made. With each passing day life in the villa, with Tomaso steadily gaining strength, was becoming steadily more familiar to her—was less traumatic.

At some point, she knew, she would need to go back to Wharton—but not quite yet. Tomaso was stronger, but he was still confined to his bed, still visibly weak—and still so grateful that she was there. His eyes would light every time she came to see him, and he would hold his hand out to her.

He asked her about Wharton, but she spoke only in general terms, not about the expenses she faced. She didn't want him offering to bankroll her. Sneering thoughts about back-payment for child maintenance were gone now—and anyway, she knew her maternal grandfather would never have accepted money from the Viales.

Her days passed lazily. There was an indoor swimming pool at the villa, and the extensive grounds were beautiful to walk around in, yet as the time passed, leisured and unhurried, eventually she grew more anxious to return to Wharton. The mortgage needed to be finalised and repairs scheduled, and Laura was eager to get stuck into all the work waiting for her.

She tackled her grandfather about the subject one afternoon, as they played chess in the library.

'I really do need to go home soon,' she said.

His eyes flickered. 'I had hoped you would come to see your place here with me as home, child,' he answered.

Dismay filled her. How could she say no—and yet how could she possibly say yes?

Tomaso saw her reaction and pressed on. 'Wait at least until Allesandro returns—he will be here for the weekend. He will have business to discuss with me of a nature very important to him.'

There was nothing she could say to that, either. She had no wish to see Allesandro di Vincenzo again, or to hear about his ambitions to run the company himself, but it seemed rude to say so to her grandfather.

'All right,' she conceded. 'But then I really must go.'

'Good, good,' said Tomaso. He reached for the chess set. 'Now, I will tell you what mistakes you made so that you can learn for the next game. You should never lose any game you play, Laura. Always play to win! I have done that all my life— and I have never lost. Not once! Whatever game I've played. And the reason is—in life as in chess—I plan ahead. Always I plan ahead—make the moves I need to make—and then I win!'

He smiled, and it seemed to Laura that it was a particularly satisfied smile. She found herself wondering why it should be— then her attention was recalled to her shortcomings at chess, and the thought slipped away from her.

Moodily, Allesandro helped himself to a flute of champagne from the tray of a circulating waiter and let his thoughts darken. His mind was not on the lunch party he was attending. It was on the fact he still was not chairman of Viale-Vincenzo. Tomaso still had not resigned. Resentment and anger burned in him. Tomaso was taking him for a ride—and it was one he did *not* appreciate.

Allesandro had thought his mood would improve when he returned to Rome. Not only would he be well out of range of both Tomaso and his repellent and graceless granddaughter, but he had also been looking forward to enjoying Delia's company again. However, when he had arrived at her apartment she had casually informed him that she was moving on.

'I'm off to the Grenadines,' she had cooed. 'Guido Salvatore's invited me to his yacht party there. I'm flying out tonight.'

Allesandro glowered into his glass as he took a large slug of the vintage champagne, hoping it would give him the buzz he needed to lighten his mood. On top of all the silence he was getting from Tomaso, he was also resenting another night of celibacy.

'Sandro, *ciao*—'

His thoughts interrupted, Allesandro acknowledged the greeting—but without pleasure. Luc Dinardi had wanted Delia Dellatore for himself, and would not miss the opportunity to offer false sympathy for her defection. He braced himself for the jibe.

But when it came, it was not about Delia's desertion.

Luc's eyes glinted with friendly malice. 'So tell me, Sandro— do I offer commiserations or congratulations? The press seem to think the latter, but then they're always hopelessly sentimental. The reality's usually different.'

Allesandro stared, frowning. What the hell was Luc talking about? The other man took a mouthful of his own champagne, his expression taunting.

'Perhaps it's a case of congratulations *and* commiserations. Congratulations on finally getting what you're after. Commiserations—' his tone changed to a humorous one '—on the way you've had to get it.' He clapped a hand on Allesandro's shoulder. 'So, when do we get to meet her?'

Allesandro's voice was blank, 'Meet who?'

Luc grinned. 'Oh, come on, Sandro—don't play coy. Your fiancée—Tomaso Viale's long-lost granddaughter.'

CHAPTER FIVE

As HIS car ate up the miles on the autostrada Allesandro's hands gripped the steering wheel as tightly as if he'd been throttling Tomaso.

But what the hell would throttling him achieve?

As little as denying it would achieve. He had known that in the split second after Luc had dropped his bombshell, and it had taken every piece of self-control he had possessed not to do so.

Because the galling truth was that he could see exactly why it was such a fascinating proposition—as the nauseating article in that morning's tabloid which Allesandro had immediately tracked down took glutinous pains to point out. It had been written in an oleaginous simper, speculating that, according to 'reliable sources', the freewheeling days of one of Rome's most eligible bachelors would soon be drawing to a close. There was a photograph of himself, at some business function, and then beside it two more photos—one of Delia Dellatore, thoughtfully pointing out that she was now in the Caribbean, as a guest of a wealthy banker, and another simply showing the blacked-out silhouette of a woman imprinted with a large question mark.

'Who is Allesandro's mystery fiancée?' posed the caption.

Then there was a final photograph. Stefano Viale, looking dashing at the helm of a powerboat—a sombre reference to his tragic death earlier that year—followed by a coy reference to a mysterious daughter. Was *this* the explanation of the mystery fiancée?

'It would be a marriage made in heaven—and in the boardroom of Viale-Vincenzo,' trilled the final words of the article, which also pointed out that it was imminently expected that Tomaso Viale would be stepping down from the chairmanship of the company, naming Allesandro di Vincenzo as his replacement.

Allesandro had forced himself to read the entire thing.

He knew exactly how it had got there. Who the 'reliable source' was. There was no other candidate for it.

His fury was incandescent, and it was still at exactly the same pitch when he strode into Tomaso's library. An eyeblink took in the scene. Tomaso in a wheelchair, before a roaring fire, playing chess with Laura Stowe.

In the same eyeblink he registered something that just for a moment diverted his rage.

The girl was smiling. Smiling at Tomaso.

He'd never seen her smile. As he stared, momentarily something else registered in his mind. She looked different when she smiled.

It was the same difference he'd seen in the car, on the way back from the hospital. But more so.

It changed the proportions of her face. Gave her something she hadn't had before—animation. Oh, he'd seen emotion in her face—cussed ill-temper!—but this animation was different. It lifted her face, lightened her heavy features. Made her look almost—

'Ah,' said Tomaso, cutting right through Allesandro's momentary confusion and focussing his irate attention back where it belonged—which was not on Laura Stowe, but on her pernicious, meddling grandfather! 'Here you are. Come and sit down. Laura, excuse us, won't you? I have some business to discuss with Allesandro.'

Tomaso seemed not in the least surprised to see him, and Allesandro knew perfectly well why. His rage intensified.

Laura got to her feet. As she'd taken in Allesandro's entrance the smile had vanished from her face as if a switch had been pulled.

'Of course,' Allesandro heard her say in a strangulated voice.

She glanced at him in stony blank-faced acknowledgement, walked right by him.

Was she in on this?

The thought seared through Allesandro's incensed brain. Then his eyes flashed back to Tomaso. And narrowed.

He was calmly, very calmly, checkmating his opponent on the chessboard with the figure he held in his fingers.

It was his queen.

Laura clumped upstairs. She was glad to be out of there. Whatever had happened, Allesandro di Vincenzo looked ready to kill over it. She didn't want to be anywhere near him, but for a moment she wondered whether she ought to go back. Whatever the cause of his anger, Tomaso was an old man—and his heart was frail. Yet he hadn't looked frail when Allesandro had stormed in. If anything, she realised with a slight frown, he'd looked—anticipatory.

Well, it was none of her business. If there was going to be a row—and there was every sign there would be!—she wanted to be well away.

Though it was drawing to the end of a damp afternoon, there was still ample time for a swim before dinner. Would Allesandro be staying for dinner? Well, that wasn't anything to do with her either.

As she came back downstairs again with her swimming things, she could hear through the partially open library door Allesandro's raised voice, speaking angry, rapid Italian. She hurried past.

In the library, Allesandro's fury with Tomaso was open.

'How *dare* you do what you did?' he demanded. 'Leak that farrago to the press! What the hell for?'

Tomaso sat back, completely unfazed.

'To force your hand, of course. Because I want the world to think you are marrying my granddaughter.'

'Are you mad?' Incredulity mixed with fury.

Tomaso's eyes rested on him. They were clear, and painfully honest.

'Not mad. Realistic.' He gave a heavy sigh and shook his head. 'Allesandro, do you think me blind when I look at her? How can I be? However dear she is to me—whatever her intelligence, or the virtues of the person she is—which are considerable—men will always judge her on the way she looks.' Was there a reprimand in his voice? Allesandro ignored it if there was—Laura Stowe's intelligence and character were irrelevant to this exchange.

Tomaso was ploughing on, his face still grave. 'So I have to ask myself the brutal question—who else will marry her, looking as she does? You, Allesandro, are the only man to have a reason to do so. To unite the two families of Viale and Vincenzo.'

The line of Allesandro's cheekbone bleached.

'Thank you for the insult,' he said softly. Dangerously.

But Tomaso only waved an impatient hand.

'It is the way the world goes round—do not be naïve! Peasants marry for parcels of land—the rich marry for shareholdings. It is understood and accepted! And don't look down your aristocratic nose at me, Allesandro!' he went on sharply. 'How do you imagine the nobles got their power and wealth—and kept it?'

'I, Tomaso—' Allesandro spelt out every word, his eyes dark '—work for my wealth. And I am *not* about to marry to increase it! So do not even *think* of trying to persuade me to take your granddaughter off your hands by, let us say, reminding me that Stefano's block of voting shares—which I understand have reverted to you now—would make an excellent dowry!'

'*Basta!*' Tomaso's eyes sparked. 'You are making assumptions that have no ground in truth. I have no desire for Laura to be landed with you as a husband.'

'Then I repeat—what the *hell* do you think you are playing at by starting these damned rumours?'

For a moment Tomaso did not answer. Then he said, 'It is a means of keeping her here in Italy. You see, she wants to go back to England. To bury herself once more. I don't mean to let that happen. I've only just discovered her—and I want her to have a reason to stay. These rumours will provide that reason.'

Allesandro leant forward. His height towered menacingly over the figure in the wheelchair.

'You want *her* to think I want to marry her?' Incredulity mingled with distaste in his voice.

'No. I want her to have a reason to go to Rome with you.'

'Excuse me? You want *me* to take her to Rome?'

'Yes. Take her about. Parties, shopping—that kind of thing. So she can get a taste of the kind of life she can have if she stays here with me, instead of taking herself off to England to bury herself in mud!'

Allesandro's voice was very controlled. 'Take her to Rome yourself, Tomaso.'

'She would not go,' the older man answered immediately. 'She would refuse.'

'And just why—' Allesandro's voice was even more controlled, his whole body was controlled '—do you imagine she would agree to go with me?'

Tomaso's eyes glinted. 'Oh, I am sure you will find a way to convince her. You are so very convincing with the ladies, are you not?'

'And why, just *why*, would I wish to convince her?'

Tomaso leant back in his wheelchair, his expression bland. Studiedly bland. A chill ran down Allesandro's spine.

'Because I have written my letter of resignation as chairman of Viale-Vincenzo, recommending your appointment to that office,' said Tomaso. 'You may have a copy if you wish.' The expression became blander yet. 'I should point out, however, that it is post-dated. A sensible precaution, don't you agree?'

Allesandro felt his jaw tighten to snapping point. 'There is only one thing on which we can agree, Tomaso, and that is that you are a—' He broke off. Fury would get him nowhere.

Tomaso was drawing an envelope from beneath the chessboard. Silently he proffered it to Allesandro. 'This is the last task I will set you,' Tomaso murmured. 'You have my word.'

His face set, Allesandro ignored the letter. Instead, he turned on his heel and walked out.

* * *

It was raining. A cold, chill rain. But Allesandro neither noticed nor cared. He was crunching along the gravelled paths around the villa in the gathering dusk. It had been raining that godforsaken day he'd had to track down Laura Stowe in her sodden, decaying wreck. The coincidence in the weather seemed appropriate.

The damn girl was quite clearly to be the bane of his life! Anger and resentment burned in him. He had been set up—completely and comprehensibly.

But not for the reasons Tomaso imagined.

His face darkened in the stinging rain. He would not forgive Tomaso for this. To renege on his word about handing over the chairmanship had been one thing, but this—this was quite another.

And it had nothing to do with the damned chairmanship of Viale-Vincenzo! This was an insult he would never forgive Tomaso for! Even though Tomaso seemed to be completely oblivious to what he had done. He had blithely talked about it being the way the world went round, as though that made it excusable, but it had put Allesandro in a quite impossible position! Rage knotted inside Allesandro as he faced what Tomaso had done to him. It was stark—blunt. He spelt it out to himself in his head, loud and clear, so there could be no mistake about it.

By starting the rumour in the press, Tomaso had ensured with bitter inevitability that the moment either a photo, or Laura Stowe herself, appeared in public—and it was inevitable that at some point one would now the press were on to her—he, Allesandro di Vincenzo, incoming chairman of Viale-Vincenzo, would be instantly condemned as a man prepared to stoop to one of two despicable acts.

To marry an ugly woman for commercial game.

Or repudiate her as too ugly to marry.

His eyes flashed with fury. *Thank you, Tomaso—thank you so much....*

It was an insult he would never forgive.

And a trap that had already been sprung.

* * *

Allesandro could feel the explosive tension mount in him again as the impossibility of his situation lashed at him. He had to discharge it somehow—anyhow! This headstrong walk through the rain was nowhere near enough. He needed hard, punishing exercise—something to release the pressure. But what? He turned the corner of the villa so that he was looking at the large, ornate glass extension. It housed the winter pool—and the gym. His pace quickened. That was what he would do—now, and urgently. Before he exploded!

As he walked rapidly past the extension towards the garden doors, he glanced inside. Someone was in the water, he registered, first with annoyance and then with puzzlement. Who the hell was in the pool? It was hard to tell through the steamed-up glass, but he could see someone getting out at the far end. It was a woman. He could just see that. She had her back to him, and she had a tail of long dark hair, slicked back by the water.

He stopped, arrested. She also had a figure to stop traffic.

The bathing suit was nothing—dark blue and sporty. He dismissed that. It covered most of her back, but it didn't need to reveal her flesh—her figure did all the work. She was standing on the shallow step leading out of the pool, her arms reaching up to wring out her hair. The gesture, lengthening the line of her body, accentuated her curves and, best of all, brought into view a tantalising glimpse through the blurred glass of her uplifted breasts. He paused, watching with instinctive masculine pleasure as she headed out of the pool area, her lissom figure still on display until she disappeared.

Who the hell was she? Enlightenment came to him. It must obviously be one of the female household staff. Tomaso was not an ungenerous employer, and perhaps allowing his senior staff the run of the gym and pool was a perk of their jobs.

He started walking again, averting his eyes from the lit interior of the pool area, glad that the pool was deserted now. Gaining entrance through the French windows, he rapidly stripped off his clothes, tossed them onto a lounger, and then, standing perfectly poised, prepared to execute a dive into the water.

* * *

Laura could feel water still trickling down her neck as she emerged from the changing room behind the pool, a towelling bathrobe over her wet bathing suit. She would shower properly in her room, and stay there till dinner. She did not want to run into Allesandro di Vincenzo again before she absolutely had to.

It had been a shock to see him again. Not because he was not expected, but because her reaction to him had not been expected.

She knew he was ridiculously good-looking—had known that from the moment he'd arrived at Wharton. And she'd seen enough of him since arriving here, in the time she'd had to spend with her grandfather in hospital, to have that no-brainer judgement amply reinforced. Allesandro di Vincenzo was God's gift to women, and that was that. Female mouths would fall open wherever he went.

Except, for obvious reasons, hers.

So why, then, when he'd stalked up to her grandfather in the library, and she had lifted her eyes to look at him, had it felt as if her stomach had suddenly ceased to exist?

It was ludicrous! Idiotic! Disturbing…

Her stomach lurched again. It was also excruciatingly embarrassing. She had no business thinking of him in that way. If he knew, it would embarrass him as much as it embarrassed her—if not more. It was completely out of place for a woman like her to pay any attention to a man who could—and doubtless did—have the pick of the most beautiful women around.

From nowhere, her imagination suddenly pictured a woman, curvaceous and sultry, undulating towards him.

He must have a fantastic body underneath those fancy suits and pristine shirts…tall and lean, and honed with a feline grace that would be like a leopard—powerful and lithe.

She stopped dead. Out of nowhere, her foetid imagination had just crashed head-first into reality. It was a head-on collision and it sent whiplash juddering through her as she stopped in the archway that opened off the array of changing cabanas.

Allesandro was standing at the edge of the pool, clearly about to dive in.

He was stark naked.

For a second—a frozen, eternal second—Laura couldn't move. Then, as if released from an arrow, the muscles of his naked body suddenly flexed, and he arched forward, entering the water in a perfect dive. For the space of a handful more seconds she saw his blurred figure dolphin-like beneath the water, then he broke the surface and surged away down the length of pool in a fast, powerful freestyle, scattering water droplets like showers of diamonds.

He powered down to the end of the pool, then twisted over to turn, his long legs flexing his spine, before breaking the surface again. And heading back down towards her.

She lurched past the archway opening to the pool as if she had been pushed by a trip hammer. Oh, God, she had to get out of here before he could catch a sight of her standing there like a total idiot! Embarrassment caught up with her, and she felt her face flame, even though no one—thank heavens!—could see it as she hurried up to gain the sanctuary of her room. She lurched into the bathroom, cheeks still flaming. There was only one mercy—he hadn't seen her gawping at him.

And I've got to pretend I never saw him! Got to erase the image from my mind! I mustn't think about it—mustn't remember it!

But it was impossible. Impossible, as she threw off her robe, peeled off her wet swimsuit and stepped under a pounding hot shower, to forget having seen him in the flesh.

All his flesh...

Despite the heat of the water, a disturbing shiver went through her. How many naked men had she seen in her life? Probably none. Not outside films or photos—and it wasn't exactly something she made a habit of studying! OK, she knew male anatomy—knew what a male body looked like—but in theory only.

Allesandro's fantastic, incredible male body was the complete and absolute opposite of theory.

She shivered again, and grabbed the soap.

It was a mistake. Suddenly, out of nowhere, she was instantly, totally aware of her own nakedness. Her own female form.

She shut her eyes and put the soap back without washing herself. She wasn't dirty anyway—just wanted to get the pool water off her. She reached for the shampoo instead, and started to wash her hair. Vigorously, roughly.

As if punishing herself.

Punishing herself for having seen what she had no business having seen—no business at all.

Allesandro di Vincenzo—clothed or unclothed—was absolutely nothing to do with her at all.

CHAPTER SIX

DINNER was an extremely strained affair. Laura wondered why Allesandro had stuck around—especially after his explosive exchange earlier with Tomaso. The two of them were carrying on a conversation in Italian, which must presumably be about business, but although Allesandro's voice was terse there were no further explosions. As for herself, she just got on with eating, wishing she had a book to read. Every now and then she would catch Allesandro's eyes on her. They seemed more baleful than she remembered.

And more disturbing.

But she crushed her reaction ruthlessly. It was as pointless as it was embarrassing.

The end of the meal could not come soon enough, and she escaped to her room with relief—especially when she heard the voices in the dining room sharpen again.

The following morning she had breakfast in her room, and then, because the rain had given way to sunshine, went for a brisk walk. She had decided that she would book her flight home today, but when she came back indoors, she was told that her grandfather wanted to see her.

'Ah, my dearest child, there you are,' he greeted her genially. Whatever altercation had taken place with Allesandro the night before, her grandfather's mood was now excellent again. 'You have been incarcerated here at the villa so long, so patiently tending to an old invalid like me! So now that the sun is finally shining, it is perfect weather to see a little of our beautiful countryside. Allesandro has agreed to take you for a drive to show you around . Yes, yes—I insist! Now, hurry. He is waiting for you in that monstrous car of his!'

Despite her immediate dismay, it was impossible—bar outright refusal—to get out of it. The last thing she wanted was to be lugged out on a sightseeing jaunt with Allesandro di Vincenzo, and his lack of enthusiasm was obvious as she walked out, to see him already seated at the wheel of a low-slung, growling black sports car. He glanced at her, blank-faced, his eyes covered by a pair of sunglasses. She clumped around to the passenger seat and got in, fumbling for her seat belt. At the front door, Tomaso was waving them goodbye cheerfully. Reluctantly she gave a half-wave back.

The car roared off in a spray of gravel, turning out of the villa's drive onto the main road and accelerating away. Did Allesandro always drive like this, or was his mood especially bad today?

She didn't care, and settled back to enjoy the ride and watch the countryside. She had paid it scant attention when she'd arrived, wound up with tension and resentment as she'd been. Now, after so long in the villa, beautiful though it was, it was good, she realised, to get out and about again—especially, she thought with a little pang, now that she was about to leave for England. She asked no questions about where they were going, nor did she attempt to make idle conversation. She just sat back and stared out of the windows at the passing landscape.

It was indeed very beautiful, and she would, she realised, miss Italy when she returned home. But she would come out again, she told herself rallyingly, to visit her grandfather. Perhaps later in the year, when the bulk of the work on Wharton was complete. In the meantime she would enjoy watching the cypresses and vineyards, the fields and woods, hills and valleys of the Italian countryside pass by.

They had joined an autostrada, she noticed at some point, but thought little of it until her eye caught a large green direction sign. She blinked.

'Where are we going?' she asked abruptly, turning her head sharply towards the car's driver.

Allesandro didn't bother to look at her. 'Towards Rome,' he said.

'*Rome?* That's too far just to go sightseeing!'

'We are not going that far,' he replied.

'But—' she began, then fell silent. She didn't care where they were going. She didn't want to be here. She was only here because Tomaso had manoeuvred her into it. She went back to staring around her.

Allesandro was glad of her silence. It left him to his own thoughts, and they were knotting him more and more tightly. His fingers gripped around the curve of the driving wheel; his foot pushed hard on the accelerator. But nothing could get him out of the trap that Tomaso had sprung. Except what he was attempting now.

He had spent the night trying to find another way out of the situation he faced. It had driven from his mind all his former concerns about the chairmanship—which right now he would willingly have renounced just to be out of this infernal impasse.

Tomaso was manipulating him yet again—and this time it was over something far more important than who ran Viale-Vincenzo. Allesandro's face darkened. His situation was intolerable. *Intolerable.*

Because this was personal.

Thanks to Tomaso, he was being made to look like a complete—

His mind veered away from the word that best suited a man prepared to marry a woman like Laura Stowe just to ingratiate himself with her grandfather, or a man who told the world by his repudiation of the rumour that she was a woman no man could stomach for a wife! Either way, he'd end up looking like a total—

No! Don't say it—don't think it! Because it's not going to happen. You're going to do the only thing you can do, and spring that damn trap Tomaso's boxed you in with. The only thing you can do...

Even as he said the words in his head, he could hear his own voice shooting them down.

You don't really think it's going to work, do you? It can't possibly work! It's hopeless. Pointless. It would take a miracle to make it work, and they're thin on the ground these days!

Stupidly, he allowed himself to glance sideways at her as she sat staring at the passing countryside. It was a mistake. Even as he took her in, sitting there like a sack of potatoes, his heart fell. *Dio*, it was hopeless—quite, quite hopeless! He might as well throw in the towel now.

Except that he would not. He would not allow his honour to be impugned in the way that Tomaso had made inevitable—to be vilified either as a man prepared to marry merely to advance his fortune, or to prove himself so shallow that he would refuse to marry a woman not stunningly beautiful. Either way, he would come out of it looking despicable.

Unless...

His jaw clenched. The 'unless' was all that was possible.

Though only a madman would put any money on it at all.

Grimly, he drove on. There was, he knew, no alternative.

'Where are we?'

Laura was staring around her. They'd come off the autostrada a while back, and now Allesandro's ferocious monster of a car was paused outside a large house set in its own grounds. It didn't have the look of a private residence. Was it some kind of hotel he'd brought her to for lunch? Her lips pressed together. If so, she didn't want to have lunch with him. Certainly not at some swanky place like this.

Allesandro took a deep breath. He hadn't been looking forward to this moment, and now that it had arrived it was worse than ever. But it had to be done. There was no alternative.

'It's a health clinic—a spa if you like. One of those places women go to have stuff done to them. God knows why, but they're very popular.' He paused minutely, then said it. 'You've been booked in for the day.'

Even as he said it, he threw a glance at the woman sitting beside him. Her heavy beetle-browed face had that suet look about it again, with eyes like gimlets, and her shoulders were hunched. Her hair was bunched up at the back of her head, like it always was. She was wearing exactly the same clothes she'd been wearing the day before. Some sort of hideous dark green tweed skirt, thick stockings, her usual clumpy shoes and a beige pullover that bagged over her shapeless figure.

Hell, why was he even bothering?

'No.'

It was just one word, but it was said with a negation that was absolute.

Her hands clenched in her lap.

'I am not going in there. Take me back to my grandfather's.'

Her voice was clipped, terse. Adamant.

Allesandro rested his hands on the wheel. He would not let them grip it the way they urged him to do.

'Your grandfather is no longer at his villa. He is going to take the waters as part of his convalescence. While he is there, he wants you to go to Rome with me. Meet people. Go to parties. Have some fun.'

Even as he said the last three words he knew he had not managed to keep the sarcasm out of them. Her eyes gored into him like the horns of a bull.

'It's what your grandfather wants,' Allesandro said tightly. 'And if you don't like it, tough. This isn't about you—it's about him. He's an old, sick man, and he wants the best for you. And you'll do it. Believe me, you'll do it.'

He paused a moment. She was looking at him as if she was the Medusa, turning all comers to stone.

'No,' she said again. One word, but it carried in it a tonne of weight, like some kind of ultra-dense element on another planet.

Allesandro felt his fingertips start to curve tensingly around the wheel. With absolute control he made them relax again. Made himself say, his voice totally neutral, 'In which case, you can repay the loan I made you. The one that got you out to Italy in the first place.'

There was a moment of absolute silence. Then, 'You didn't say it was a loan.' Her voice was stretched. Stretched fine.

He didn't care.

He saw the change in her eyes. Saw it, and didn't care. Didn't give a single tinker's curse. He had one goal now, one only: to get the woman sitting beside him inside those damn doors. Any way he could. Including this.

'It was in the small print. A whole page of it, actually. The entire sum is repayable at any time of my choosing.'

Memory floated in front of Laura's eyes. The contents of the envelope that had arrived…the letter…the cheque…the piece of paper written in closely typed Italian…

She stared at him. Hatred boiled in her. More than hatred. Worse than hatred.

The knowledge was like a box closing in on her. That there was absolutely nothing she could do. Nothing.

Except what he wanted of her.

But I can't—I just can't! I can't go in there and…

The hot, horrible tide of mortification swept through her. Almost she cried out aloud—*Don't make me! Please, please don't make me go in there!*

The cruelty of it was unbearable.

But she would have to bear it. Even as the words formed in her mind she felt the hot, flushing tide sink down again. Replaced by cold ice-water filling every vein, numbing her.

And that was good. That was essential. She needed to be numb now. Needed to become a sleepwalker. A zombie. Not there inside her head at all.

Jerkily, she got out of the car. She would feel nothing. She would be a martyr going to her fate. Bowing her head to the mockery of the jeering crowds.

I can bear this. I can bear it because I have no alternative. I

*haven't got the money to repay that loan. I can't go to Tomaso—
I just can't. Because he thinks, God help me, that this hideous
ordeal I'm going to have to go through is actually something I
might want! Something I might welcome.*

Hollowness caved within her. Tomaso wouldn't realise how
cruel he was being, she knew that. She knew he was doing what
he thought would be some kind of treat for her—some kind of gift!

Her grandparents—her mother's parents—had known better.
They had known she was a lost cause, that nothing could be done.
They'd tried only once. The bitter, humiliating memory assailed
her. She'd been eighteen, and her grandparents had, on one of
their rare excursions from their reclusive lifestyle, gone to the
local hunt ball, taking her with them. Her grandmother had spent
ages helping her choose an evening gown—her very first—
taking her to a hairdresser in the local market town, helping her
with her make-up.

Even as she remembered now, years later, Laura could feel
again the stinging, burning mortification she had felt that awful,
awful evening. Knowing instantly, as they'd walked in, that she
looked a fright. She hadn't needed to hear the smothered giggles
from the other girls there, to see the instantly dismissive looks
on the young men's faces…

She felt again that flood of mortification—felt it, and smothered it. She wasn't eighteen any more. She was an adult, with
adult responsibilities, and overriding one was to Wharton.

With feet of lead, she walked inside.

Ready to face her nightmare.

Allesandro gunned the engine and roared off down the private
road of the health spa. What the hell had he gone and done?
Drastic cosmetic surgery and six months' starvation would
hardly be enough to transform *this* woman! The clinic had a
handful of hours. At eight-thirty that evening he would be
walking into Christa Bellini's charity reception at the Hotel
Montefiore in Rome—where just about everyone he knew would
also be—and the farce would begin.

Can I go through with it? Can I really go through with it?

His foot pressed down on the accelerator. Yes, he could go through with it. If he wanted to emerge from Tomaso's trap looking anything other than a total louse, he would have to go through with it. Even with the odds stacked so heavily against him.

Damn the girl! She was nothing but a total, absolute nuisance! OK, none of this was her fault. But if she simply hadn't existed, *none* of this unholy mess would have happened.

Bitterly, he headed into Rome. He would bury himself in work and do everything he could to stop himself thinking of the ordeal awaiting him.

'This way, Signorina Stowe.'

The elegantly chic woman leading the way spoke fluent, accented English. Laura clumped after her. Her face was expressionless.

It stayed expressionless for the next seven hours. It was the only way she could get through the endless, interminable, pointless things that were done to her. Every now and then something inside her wanted her to jump to her feet, yell at all the people doing those things, tell them it was all totally, utterly a waste of their time and skill. Yell at them to leave her alone. For pity's sake, to just *leave her alone*!

But she couldn't. It would have been unthinkable. Rude. Discourteous. Unforgivable.

And besides, she was in a trap and she couldn't get out of it. There was no point thinking otherwise. She just had to go through with it—the same way she got through life all the time. Knowing, wherever she went, that she was what she was. Nothing was going to change that. Not a haircut, nor facial treatments, or any of the other endless, complex, incomprehensible processes she was subjected to, hour after hour. And certainly not new clothes.

Laura suddenly had a searing memory of being with her grandmother in the market town's only boutique, excitedly choosing that evening dress. She remembered being fondly guided by her grandmother, relying on her, because she'd never bought an evening dress before. Then, remembered, with bleak pain, how for the only time in her life a new emotion had filled her.

Hope. Hope that some kind of miracle would happen. That a new hairstyle, a new dress, some make-up would achieve the transformation that she had longed for.

And then came the memory of the hideous, bitter, dull, burning anguish of realising, as she'd walked into that hunt ball, just how futile that hope had been.

Her grandparents had known, but had said nothing. And never again had Laura tried to escape the destiny she saw every time she looked in a mirror.

I am what I am. It's not a crime. It's not a vice. It's not a weakness. It's a fact of life. That's all. So don't make a fuss about it.

She wasn't making a fuss now. She was just sitting there, lying there, doing what she was being told to do, letting the team of non-stop attendants do what they wanted, taking relieved refuge in being English and using that as an excuse not to talk. Not to participate. It would only be polite to do so, she knew. And she felt for all the people working on her. They would be polite, and if she let them she knew they would make kind, encouraging remarks to her. But she didn't want that. Didn't want kindness or encouragement. Not when all they were really expressing was the one thing she did not want—pity.

So she just bowed her head and endured.

Eventually, after what seemed a lifetime, it was finally all over. It had grown dark outside, and the blinds covering the windows had been drawn. The last of the endless applications of gunk on her hair, face and body had been removed. She'd had a final shower, a final body cream massage, and then been wrapped in a soft bathrobe. Her hair had been styled, her face made-up, and her brand-new artificial nails painted. It had been the state of her hands and nails that had aroused the most audible exclamations of horror, and Laura had remembered Allesandro's similar comments when they had first met.

Now she was being put into underwear—so wispy it was hardly there—and then into stockings so sheer they were almost invisible. Finally a dark blue gown was carefully lowered over her head, thankfully long-sleeved, and with a boat-shaped neckline, but it still felt distressingly tight on her. Her feet were slid into high-heeled shoes, and she was presented with a dark blue evening bag. Only then was she ushered from the thankfully mirrorless room.

At the door, Laura paused and turned. The team of beauticians and stylists looked at her expectantly.

She knew she had to say something; they'd worked on her for hours. They deserved some acknowledgement from her, but when she spoke she said only one thing—the only thing it made sense to say.

'*Mi dispiace.* I'm sorry.'

One of the beauticians said something in low Italian to another, who gave a low laugh. Laura felt a flush spear across her cheekbones.

It was starting already.

The sniggering.

For a split second she felt overcome by a powerful urge to tear the dress from her body and demand her old clothes back. Then she would find a taxi, go to the airport and get back to England, to Wharton, on the first plane out of Italy.

I can't go through with this—I just can't! Please, please don't make me!

Claws of dread and mortification hooked viciously at her stomach.

Then her spine stiffened. She wouldn't run! She wouldn't. She could do this. After all, she was only going to have to face strangers. That was all. Even Tomaso would not be there to witness what was going to happen.

The only person she was going to see tonight would be Allesandro di Vincenzo—and what did she care about him?

Nothing. Nothing at all. He'd made his opinion of her crystal-clear. She knew the revulsion she'd seen in his eyes, and what did she care about it? Nothing.

Like a martyr going to her doom, she straightened her shoulders, lifted her chin, turned, and strode from the room.

CHAPTER SEVEN

ALLESANDRO sat at the bar of the Hotel Montefiore in a fashionable part of Rome, nursing a beer, his mood dark. Any time now his ordeal was about to start. In one of the hotel's grand function rooms, just across the spacious mezzanine lobby, the other guests were already gathering.

He was waiting for his partner for the evening.

Laura Stowe.

Dio, of all females in the world! Laura Stowe.

The minutes were ticking by. He'd sent a car to the clinic to collect the girl, and she would be here at any moment. For an instant he wished he'd had the guts to go and get her himself—that way he would have known the worst before they got here and it became too late. But he'd been caught up in work at the office, and he'd ended up with insufficient time to get back to his apartment and change. So instead he was stuck here, waiting for her to be delivered to him.

He took another mouthful of beer. Maybe he should phone the clinic. Ask them bluntly what he needed to know—

Just how bad is it?

But what was the point? He'd find out at any moment. And after all, however bad it was, it could not be worse than it had been before he'd handed her into the place. It just couldn't be!

Or could it? Into his head crawled a saying, cruel and vicious—and true.

No point putting lipstick on a pig...

He pushed his beer glass away sharply, forcing the words out of his head.

And suddenly, out of nowhere, he knew with absolute certain decision that he could not go through with this plan. He couldn't do it to her.

Laura Stowe might be obstinate, unpleasant, ungracious, with a personality he wouldn't wish on anyone, but there were some things no decent man could do to a woman. This was one of them.

The odds against this plan succeeding—the only plan possible, given the box that Tomaso had nailed him into—were so high that it had been pointless even entertaining them! The outcome was obvious—inescapable. This idiotic gamble could not possibly come off—which meant that what would happen would be just too brutally cruel for any man—including him, driven as he was—to subject any girl to.

I can't make her the object of mockery—not even of pity. I can't do it to her.

Resolution steeled through him. There was no way he was going to expose Laura Stowe in front of Roman society to be looked down on or pitied for being so ugly. He simply wouldn't do it.

As for himself—well, tough. Today's tabloids had run *en masse* with the canard that Tomaso had so deviously fed them, whipping up yet more juicy speculative gossip that he was about to cement his control of Viale-Vincenzo with a highly advantageous marriage to Tomaso's granddaughter. But what they hadn't printed was that the granddaughter in question was a woman whom, on the basis of looks alone, no one would marry *without* the marriage being very, very advantageous.

There had been only one way open to him to spike those guns aimed at him from both invidious directions. To present the world with a granddaughter that no one would need bribing to marry...

But what chance was there of that? He faced up to it grimly. When Laura Stowe turned up here, nothing, absolutely nothing, would have changed. However much lipstick she wore...

And he just couldn't do it to her. No way. End of story.

So he'd just take the flak that came. Laura wanted to get back to England, and Allesandro decided that he'd happily pack her off there tomorrow, now that Tomaso was out of the picture. As for himself, when at some point everyone drew their own conclusion—that he'd turned down Tomaso Viale's granddaughter because she wasn't fit to be the bride of so discerning a connoisseur of female beauty as Allesandro di Vincenzo—well, he would just tough that out too. He would come across like a shallow, conceited jerk, but, hell, he could take it.

Laura Stowe couldn't.

After all, she'd taken enough...

His mouth compressed. OK, she had a spiky, grouchy personality, and she wasn't gracious or charming, but after all, he allowed, she hadn't had the easiest ride in the world. She had grown up knowing that her father had never wanted her or her mother, and yet for all that she'd made peace with her grandfather, stood by him when he'd needed him. Allesandro also acknowledged that she had principle enough not to regard Tomaso as a banker to pay for her derelict house, or indeed to regard him as a golden meal ticket. But most of all, he reminded himself, none of this infernal situation was of her making! *It wasn't her fault.*

Just as the way she looked wasn't her fault.

It couldn't be easy looking like that, especially for a woman... *And he wasn't going to make it harder. She didn't deserve that.*

Decision made, he pushed back from the bar. He'd go down to the lobby, out to the portico, wait for her car and stop her getting out. Instead of tonight's bash he'd take her somewhere quiet, where he might not be known. Where the paparazzi and the gossip hacks wouldn't be hanging out waiting to take cruel, exposing photos of Tomaso's granddaughter, to write their poisonous, hurtful words about her.

He would protect her from that if he could do nothing else. And tomorrow he'd pack her off to England, where she wanted to go anyway. Get her safely away from cruel gossip and malicious mockery.

He started to lever himself to his feet. And stopped dead.

A woman in an elegant evening dress was standing just by the bar entrance, her body slightly averted, looking towards the function rooms. Allesandro felt his gaze rivet to her like a magnet.

All thoughts of Laura Stowe vanished like ice in the sun's core. He couldn't take his eyes from the woman.

Dio, but she was something to look at! Totally something! Her body was hourglass perfect, with breasts cresting beneath a fine silk jersey that lovingly moulded each lush peak before cinching in at her waist to hug the perfectly rounded, enticing swell of her bottom and then cascade down to pool around her high-heeled shoes. The high cut of the neckline merely served to accentuate the rich curves of her body, as did the swathe of dark hair swept dramatically around one shoulder.

A *bella figura* to perfection!

Oh, yes, she was definitely, very definitely, something to look at!

For one long moment he just stood and stared at her, willing her to turn. He wanted to see her face—her body had already told him everything he wanted to know about her, but he wanted to see her face.

Who the hell was she? He hadn't seen her before, that was for sure, or he'd have been a whole lot more closely acquainted with her already! But even as his eyes narrowed speculatively there was the faintest tug of familiarity about her. He searched rapidly through his extensive mental database of women he knew and had categorised as desirable, but could not find a match. Definitely someone new on the social scene, then.

And definitely worth making a move on...

Interest flared in him—and then, like a douche of cold water, the reality check hit him like a wet rag in the face.

Dio, what the hell was he thinking of? He wasn't about to make a move on her or any other woman! Not now, and especially not tonight.

Frustration knifed through him.

He paused for one last fraction of a second, to take his final fill of her, intensely reluctant to lose this moment of surveying the woman who had caught his eye so absolutely.

The woman was, at last, turning her head. But not towards him. She had changed the angle of her body and swept her head round to look into the bar area—but, frustratingly, he still could not see her face.

Something, he could tell, had caught her attention.

Allesandro twisted his head slightly to see what it was. Or who. If it was another man, he needed to know. Urgently. Even though it was pointless information in the circumstances.

But it wasn't another man who had caught her attention.

And as Allesandro realised just who it was that had—realised who it was she was staring at—he felt shock empty the breath from his lungs.

Allesandro di Vincenzo was looking at a woman. Laura could see him—and the woman in question. Only their reflections, caught in the polished steel wall of the ferociously modernist bar interior, but she knew it was him straight away.

He was impossible to miss.

Through the tightly wired mesh of the tension that was knotting her body and mind, she felt the slicing pull of a completely new source of tension.

She had known right from the very first time of setting eyes on him that Allesandro di Vincenzo was a ludicrously attractive male—but now she was seeing him in a condition that made everything that had gone before, pale into insignificance.

He looked spectacular in evening dress—and he was looking at a woman. A woman who had drawn his attention for all the reasons that any woman would want him to…

She could see why…

Even though the woman's face was averted, the rest of her was stunning. Although the mirrored steel had muted the colour of her gown to a dark, smoky shade, she could see the material was tightly sheathed to curve around her contours.

She felt that wire tug through her again. There was something about his absolute focus on the woman—his slightly narrowed eyes, the stillness of his head, the air of tension in the line of his body—that got to her. It was exactly the same sensation, she knew, with a hollowing of her insides, that had hit *her* when she had caught sight of him poised at the edge of her grandfather's swimming pool, stark naked in all his lean, incredible male silhouette.

She mustn't look at him like that! She just mustn't!

Jerkily, she broke the moment and stepped forward. Out of the corner of her eye she registered that the woman he'd been eyeballing had moved as well. Instantly Laura untwisted her neck, looking straight ahead of her instead of at the reflective wall. And as she did so, taking another jerky step forward, she stopped dead suddenly. It was the woman again, dead ahead of her. Still a smoky reflection.

But…

Rapidly Laura whipped her gaze back again—and shocking realisation dawned. The walls of the bar were angled so that two polished walls intersected, creating a duplicated reflection from a different angle. She brought her head round sharply again to the second reflection, which showed the woman again. Facing her.

Laura frowned, disorientated. Where was the woman, then? If she could see her straight ahead of her, even though she could not make out the woman's features at this distance across the length of the room, she must be standing close to her.

But there was no one else near her. Only the tall, unmistakable form of Allesandro di Vincenzo. But he was no reflection this time, he was flesh and blood.

She stared, as he had, at the figure in the reflection, and then, as if in slow motion, she saw his head twist slightly, his gaze shift around to her direction. To where the woman he had been staring at must be standing.

Right next to her.

Except that there wasn't any woman…

And then, as if in even slower motion—motion so slow it was

like a thick, viscous bubble forming inside her—she was filled with a shock so absolute it stopped the blood in her heart.

Allesandro watched her freeze—watched her with eyes that had frozen as well. It had been the reflection that had done it—the one that had showed him the woman's face, full on, from where he sat.

A reflection that emptied the breath from his lungs.

No!

Denial—absolute, incontrovertible—seared through him. No. It was not possible. It was just not possible. *Basta.* Enough. Stop.

The words were staccato in his head, repeating themselves. Without sense or meaning.

Just as what he was seeing had no sense, no meaning. Because it couldn't have. It just couldn't.

He'd looked at a woman—responded instantly, strongly, to what she had on show. But it couldn't be that woman. It just couldn't. Because the woman in the entrance to the bar was now staring at a reflection of herself. And that face—

That face belonged to a different woman.

A woman as different from the one whose figure he'd been caught by as a thrush was from a bird of paradise. A woman who, in the first moment of meeting her, he'd consigned to the waste-land of women unremittingly bereft of the slightest appeal whatsoever. So how could the woman he was staring at frozenly now be—?

It can't be her—it just can't!

The denial blitzed through his brain, blocking each synapse with impenetrable concrete. Yet even as he heard the words in his head he felt his gaze tear from the smoky reflection he could see to the actual figure standing staring at herself.

As frozen as he was.

As shocked as he was.

Shock buckled through him again as he realised why she was standing like that.

She didn't know—she didn't know it was herself.

His eyes focussed on her, taking in the expression of complete, absolute stupefaction. Disbelief.

Denial.

Almost, *almost* he gave a bark of laughter. Mordant, black. *Dio*, of course Laura Stowe did not recognise herself! No one would recognise her! No one who'd ever seen her would possibly, *possibly* think she was the woman standing there, with a figure that could stop traffic and a face—

A face that would turn heads from a hundred metres.

Another jolt of incredulity jarred through him.

Where had she gone?

Where had she gone—that suet-faced, beetle-browed, gimlet-eyed, hedge-haired, atrociously dressed lump of a female, who clumped heavily around on her heavy shoes perpetually sour-expressioned, with her thin, tight, always-so-damn-disapproving mouth and clenched jaw? Where the hell *was* she?

Because the woman who stood there, dramatically framed, lushly outlined, her rich swathe of hair swept back from one side of her face to arc across the other and then cascade around one shoulder, was nothing, *nothing* like the one he had driven away from lunchtime.

This woman had dramatic looks, with high cheekbones and a sculpted nose and jaw, with winged eyebrows that arched over eyes that were deep and wide and haunting and just amazingly luminous, and a mouth that was an incredible slash of dark scarlet.

He reeled mentally. Unable to think rationally.

How had they done it? The question tolled in his brain. How the hell had they done it? How had she been completely, absolutely remade from head to foot? As if she were a totally different person. There was nothing left of the woman she had been.

Except—

Except her complete disbelief.

Slowly, he got to his feet and walked towards her. She was still standing there, staring at her reflection, frozen in shock. He came up to her. 'You need a drink,' he said. Then added, 'So do I.' His voice sounded hollow in his ears.

He took her elbow. For a second she resisted. Not actively, but as if the act of him laying a hand on her had simply sent another shock detonating through her, rendering her incapable of anything else, let alone being guided towards the long silvered curve of the bar. Then, abruptly, she stopped resisting. Walked, instead, expression like a zombie, to gain one of the high stools aligned along the bar. She stepped up onto the stool, and as she lowered herself down Allesandro could not stop himself automatically registering the way the fine stretch material of her gown moulded afresh around her incredible figure.

It can't be her! It just can't!

Yet again denial, absolute and certain, seared through him. Two completely different women had collided in his brain, and he just could not unite them. The woman collapsed on the stool, as motionless now as if she were frozen. This *could not be* Laura Stowe.

But she was. She was Laura Stowe.

Non credo—

But he had to believe it. It was true.

'*Signor, Signorina—*'

The barman was there, hovering attentively. His eyes, Allesandro could tell immediately, had flicked from him to dwell on the woman at his side. Allesandro knew why—for the same reason that his had gone to her the moment he'd registered her presence in the entranceway. For the same reason that every male who would ever set eyes on her would turn his head to look at her...

Men turning their heads to look at Laura Stowe...

And not with revulsion...

'Brandy. Two.' He spoke shortly, having no mental energy left for words.

The glasses appeared almost instantly, filled with a generous measure. Allesandro pushed one at Laura.

'Drink,' he said. 'You need it.'

She wasn't looking at him. She was staring behind the bar. There was another mirror there, but a proper one this time, not the polished steel of the walls. This one reflected the bottles and glasses in front of it, reflected those seated at the bar. Reflected Laura Stowe.

She was transfixed, he could see. Still in quite visible shock. There was complete blankness in her face. Her eyes were distended, mouth slightly parted, as if she were finding breathing hard.

Or irrelevant.

Irrelevant was anything other than the image that was being sent back from the mirror through her eyes into her brain.

But it wasn't reaching her brain yet—Allesandro could see that. And could understand. It was barely reaching his own. The dissonance was so great, so overwhelming.

For her, he could see, it was—impossible.

'Drink,' he said again. 'Or you'll pass out.'

He pushed the glass at her fingers, at her hands laid, splayed on the surface of the bar. Hands that weren't scratched or calloused. Hands that were smooth—as smooth as the satin purse lying beside them, its shade exactly the same as that of the indigo gown that sheathed her body like a loving glove. Hands whose fingers were slender and tipped with long, elegant, lightly varnished nails.

Beautiful hands—as perfect as the rest of her...

Laura Stowe—beautiful...

Incredulity slugged through him again. With an abrupt movement he picked up his own glass and took a mouthful of the fiery liquor within. It burned down his throat, but he was glad of it. It seemed to make this outrageous reality just a tad less outrageous. A tad more real.

Laura's fingers had closed around the stem of her brandy glass. Without taking her eyes from her own reflection, she lifted it to her mouth in a jerky motion.

The brandy choked her as it went down, and she gave a sudden, rasping cough. But the motion stirred her, revived her. Let her tear her eyes away and slowly, very slowly, turn her head towards the man sitting beside her.

It was Allesandro di Vincenzo. Allesandro di Vincenzo sitting beside the woman reflected in the mirror behind the bar. The woman he'd been looking at when she'd paused by the entrance to the bar. Whom she had seen in a reflection—a double reflection. She tried to get her brain around the way she had seen the woman sideways on, seen Allesandro looking at her...

The way he was looking at her now...

Rejection seared through her.

It isn't me! It isn't me! It can't be! I can't be that woman—I just can't!

The litany of denial ran through her head, each word like a hammer.

Jerkily, she lifted the brandy glass to her lips again, took another fiery sip. This time it didn't choke her, but it seemed to kick through her like an electric current. As she lowered the glass again, she saw the edge of the glass was smudged with scarlet.

Scarlet lipstick. The same as the woman in the mirror had on...

Cold drenched through her, and then heat. There was a buzzing in her ears, a thickness in her vision. She stared blindly at the man beside her.

He blurted something sharply in Italian, which she could not understand. But then the whole world was going very fuzzy all around her.

He caught her even as she slumped, unable to stay upright as the fuzziness poured in on her. She could feel hard fingers holding her shoulders, could hear his deep, accented voice—in English now—cutting through the fog.

'Don't faint on me! Come on—clear your head. Clear it. Take a deep breath!'

She did what she was told, and slowly the world came back into focus, the fuzzed blur receding again. She pulled back, away from the hard hands that slipped from her shoulder. She stared at Allesandro blankly.

'Can you speak?' he asked. There was a mordant tone to his voice.

Laura shook her head. No, she couldn't speak. She couldn't think. She couldn't do anything. All she could was sit here and stare blankly. She watched, still blankly, as he snapped his fingers for the barman and ordered a glass of water. Then he put the glass into her nerveless fingers.

As he did so, something else registered in her numbed brain.

He was touching her. His hand was touching her. The way it had touched her elbow when he'd guided her to the seat here, the way it had cupped over her shoulder to stop her fainting away.

Allesandro was touching her…making her lift the glass to her mouth…making her sip the water slowly, swallowing each sip and taking another…holding eye contact with her so that the fuzz that was all about in the peripheral field of her stricken vision would not come rolling in again.

As she swallowed the water, sip by sip, she felt—finally—an easing of the numbness that had transfixed her ever since that moment when she'd walked into the bar area and realised, with a body-blow of extreme disbelief, just who the image was reflecting.

How did they do it? How did all those treatments do this to me? Maybe it's some kind of mask over my face—maybe it's some kind of plastic surgery that you don't feel or something…

Maybe it's a spell…

Almost, she gave a hysterical laugh. But she managed to stifle it. Hysteria was very close beneath the surface, one layer away from the shock that had taken her over so consumingly that she had almost passed out with it.

Her eyes were dragged back to the reflection behind the bar.

She saw them both instantly. Allesandro, looking exactly as he always did—breathtaking in his dinner jacket.

And the woman beside him. A woman with hands cupped around a half-drunk glass of water, gripping it as if it was an instrument of salvation. A woman with eyes so wide a face so blank that she was completely immobile.

A woman who was—

Beautiful.

She made herself say the word. Made herself say it in her head, clear, and unmistakable. Undeniable.

A woman she had thought was someone else because she could not possibly, *possibly* be her!

Blindly, she released the glass of water and reached for the brandy glass, taking another small, fiery sip. It brought the world and her image into sharper focus.

'Ready?'

She blinked, twisting her head to look at Allesandro directly. He had an enquiring look on his face.

'If you're feeling up to it now, we should be going in.'

'In?' she echoed. Her voice seemed husky.

He nodded towards the function rooms across the mezzanine lobby.

'It's what we came for, remember? Your grandfather wants you to have a social life.'

Even as he said the words another slug of shock went through him. A mental double-take in his brain.

This was Tomaso's granddaughter—the mystery granddaughter—the woman beside him! This woman who had a figure like a goddess and a face that would turn every male head who saw it!

The way she'd turned his....

No! He mustn't think of that! He must not.

He got to his feet and held out an imperious hand to the girl sitting there.

'Laura?'

He'd said her name. Even though it was impossible, just impossible—crazy, even!—to apply that name to the woman at the bar with him. Numbly she slid off her stool, and silently Allesandro handed her the evening bag. She clutched it as if she were gaining strength from it. He ushered her forward, letting her free hand clutch at his sleeve, as if that alone were keeping her upright. She walked beside him—stalked on heels that made her almost as tall as him, that lifted her hips and made him supremely, acutely, intensely aware of her presence at his side.

As they exited the bar he could feel the eyes of everyone on her, and as they crossed the lobby another thought came to him. One that sent a final debilitating shock wave through him.

The woman at his side was going to create a sensation tonight.

CHAPTER EIGHT

'ALLESANDRO! How lovely to see you!' The elegant matron who was the hostess of the charity reception inclined one lightly powdered cheek to be kissed, which office Allesandro duly performed. 'And your guest tonight is…?' Christa Bellini enquired, her smile welcoming, but piqued with curiosity.

'May I present Laura Stowe?' Allesandro said with formal courtesy.

Signora Bellini's eyes lit. 'Ah, you must be English.' She smiled at Laura, speaking in that language for her guest's benefit. 'I'm so pleased you have been able to come tonight. Have you been in Rome long?'

Somehow, Laura found a voice. Years of training by her grandparents paid off. They might have lived reclusive lives, but she knew her social duty. Even at a time when shock was still reeling in every sense in her body, every cell in her brain.

'This is my first evening,' she managed.

'Indeed? And have you known Allesandro long?'

The curiosity was open now. Polite, but definitely there.

'A little while,' she said. She was speaking like an automaton, but she couldn't help it.

'Ah, with our handsome Allesandro a little while is all it takes!' Signora Bellini said lightly, but Allesandro was well aware of the glance thrown in his direction as she spoke.

And, like a douche, of what it meant. He had introduced

Laura by her maternal name—Christa Bellini had had no reason to think her Tomaso's mystery granddaughter and every reason to think something quite, quite different. As her very next words showed.

'And of course Delia is in the Caribbean at the moment, no? With Guido Salvatore, so I understand. A little elderly, perhaps, but then again he is a widower. Who knows what comfort he may seek in his antiquity? Perhaps even a new young wife.' She gave a light laugh, and Allesandro was glad she'd reverted to Italian.

He was also glad that she was required to turn her attention to the next guests arriving. He seized Laura's arm and steered her away into the throng. He was still not in command of himself, he realised. Not functioning properly. But, given that Laura was like a zombie at his side, he knew he had to pull himself together. He was here for a purpose. He had to remember that.

And suddenly, cutting right down through the state of mush that was currently his brain, realisation hit him.

His plan—his hopeless, back-against-the-wall, no-hope plan—had worked. The staggering odds against it had come out even. Against all the cards stacked against it.

The shock wave came again. Turning his brain back to mush.

But if his brain were mush, his body was telling him something very clearly indeed. And it had absolutely everything to do with the woman at his side.

And nothing to do with who her grandfather was.

Laura could say nothing, do nothing. All she could do was walk forward, Allesandro at her side, guiding her direction. People started to talk to him, and he was drawn further into the room. A waiter circulated with a tray of champagne glasses. Allesandro handed her one, and she took small, repetitive sips from it. Another waiter circulated with canapés, but she could not take any. People said things to her—first in Italian, then in English. All she could do was look blank and nod, and take another sip of champagne. Allesandro seemed to be talking a lot. She was grateful. It seemed odd to be grateful to him.

But then 'odd' was the very least description of what she was feeling—what was happening.....

Don't think—can't think—just...just...

Just keep doing whatever it was she was doing now...

Somehow, and she had no idea how, she kept going. And as the sips of champagne went down, and her glass emptied, and another was placed in her hand, something quite extraordinary started to happen inside her.

She didn't know what it was, but it was definitely happening. It was like a bubble forming. Very slowly, very small, but getting larger—sort of swelling deep inside, welling up from nowhere. Growing inexorably, ineluctably...

Taking her over.

Someone else had come up to Allesandro. A man. Her eyes went to him. She could tell that he was about Allesandro's age. And very handsome.

He was speaking Italian to Allesandro, but he didn't even finish what he was saying before his eyes slid to her.

The bubble inside her swelled and enveloped her totally.

She met his eyes. Met them and it was like the universe suddenly changing—completely and for ever.

The man was taking her hand, lifting it to his mouth.

'Laura—' he said, and his eyes never broke from her. 'It is a pleasure to meet you.'

The way he said her name—in the Italian style, with an 'ow' sound instead of the English 'or' sound—purred in her mind..

His eyes were still holding hers—dark and long-lashed—and in them was something Laura had never, ever seen before.

Her breath caught, and her face lit with an electric smile.

She saw the man's eyes flare, and the breath in her lungs tightened.

The man closed his hands around hers, his thumb smoothing over her palm.

A caress—

There was a sharp phrase of Italian. Not from the man. From Allesandro. At once the man let go of her hand. She felt bereft.

The man glanced at Allesandro, and something flashed between them. Then Allesandro said something else, just as sharp. The man gave an elegant shrug, a smile playing at his mouth. Then, with a little bow of his head at Laura, he murmured something she could not catch and veered away. Laura felt her gaze go after him.

Her elbow was taken in a tight grip, and she was steered in the opposite direction.

'Keep clear of Luc Dinardi. He'd eat you for breakfast.'

Allesandro's voice was harsh. As if he were angry.

She looked at him. It was easier to do that now, after all those sips of champagne on top of the brandy earlier.

Allesandro stared down at her. There was incomprehension in her face. He felt exasperation jab through him. *Dio*, it was like taking a spring lamb through a pack of wolves! A lamb that didn't even know she was one! And who wouldn't recognise a wolf until there was nothing left of her but her bones!

But then, he knew she had absolutely no idea whatsoever of the impact she was having. Every man there was looking her over, and if he had not been at her side she'd have been swamped immediately. Even his presence hadn't been enough to deter Luc Dinardi, whose voracious sex-life made his own seem tame in comparison. A frown drew briefly between his brows. Luc had actually got a smile from her! His mouth tightened momentarily. The last thing Luc needed was any encouragement.

'Allesandro, won't you introduce me to your beautiful companion?'

Allesandro swivelled his head. His eyes darkened. If he'd thought Luc Dinardi a danger to keep far away, the man who was now blatantly looking over the woman at his side was even more so.

It was for more than just his lifestyle that the man in front of them had become infamous. And Allesandro knew that there was another, much more compelling reason for keeping Ernesto Arnoldi at bay. Now in late middle age, he had been a boon companion of Stefano Viale, despite the five-year gap in their ages. Both had been drawn together by their involvement in powerboat racing and other libertine proclivities. Arnoldi's wild parties on board his yacht were notorious, and Stefano had been a constant guest. He was not the kind of man to introduce to anyone as green as Tomaso's granddaughter, but short of cutting him direct Allesandro was obliged to perform the introduction.

As he did so, he was glad that Laura's surname appeared to be completely unknown to Arnoldi. But then why should it be known? Stefano had ignored her existence all his life—why would he have mentioned a rejected bastard daughter to his partner in notoriety?

To his relief, Arnoldi did nothing more than take Laura's hand, then release it.

'As ever, Allesandro, you have excellent taste,' he murmured, his heavy lidded eyes lingering on her face in a way that made Allesandro's hackles rise. Then, thankfully, he was gone, mingling back with the crowd again.

Allesandro closed his hand around Laura's elbow again. He felt her stiffen, but he didn't care. It seemed like an important gesture to make right now.

'Stay away from him, too—even more so,' he said. 'He knew Stefano, and was always a bad influence on him.'

Laura's mouth tightened. 'Two of a kind, obviously.'

Allesandro glanced at her. The familiar bite was back in her voice. If he'd shut his eyes he'd have sworn it was the same Laura Stowe he knew and disliked, even though in this instance he could hardly dispute her comment. But his eyes were not shut—they were looking at a woman who still, even now, made him disbelieve the evidence staring at him.

Two women—two completely different women…

He felt incomprehension knife through him again. The disparity between the two was so great he could not bridge it in his mind. Yet already this woman was starting to obliterate the other one. He couldn't stop it. Couldn't stop his eyes working over her stunningly dramatic face yet again, taking in the impact of her spectacular figure.

Why did it seem familiar? That incredible body—

The question nagged at him, and then, in a sudden lightning bolt of realisation, he knew. *Dio*—in the pool last night—that had been her! *Her* figure—her breasts, and waist, hips and shoulders, and fantastically proportioned legs…

She had been there all along…

There beneath those hideous clothes that she had worn to turn herself into a frump. Just as, he realised—again with that knifing of disbelief—those dramatic looks must have been there somewhere. Somehow.

Get rid of those beetle brows, style her hair, sculpt her face with make-up, deepen her eyes with shadow, lengthen her lashes with mascara, paint her mouth so you could actually see it, bring out the bones and contours that were there… She had been there all along…complete in her identity as a woman no man could possibly look on without interest.

Let alone without desire.

Immediately he cut the thought from him. *No!* Desire was absolutely not a word he could associate with the woman at his side. She was Tomaso's granddaughter. He had to remember that. It was imperative to do so.

It was just that it was extremely hard…

Yet again his eyes swept over her show-stopping figure, curved and indented in all the right places to perfection. An urge to reach out and run his hands over her fired through him.

No! Yet again he thrust the thought from him.

She's Tomaso's granddaughter. She's Laura Stowe—Laura Viale—it doesn't matter what her name is, you know who she is and you do not touch her…

You do not touch her!

But he wanted to.

He wanted to touch her, glide his hands down that fantastic body, draw her towards him…

She wasn't even looking at him. She was gazing out across the crowded room. There was less blankness in her face now—as if she was slowly, very slowly, coming out of what was obviously a state of profound shock. He knew what had done it—Luc

Dinardi coming on to her had finally seemed to awaken in her a realisation of just what kind of effect she was having on the male sex. Then there had been that swift reversion to the acid-tongued female he'd come to know—and dislike. It was something he had to remember, he cautioned himself. Laura Stowe might look transformed on the outside, but underneath she was still exactly the same acerbic-tongued female she'd always been.

His gaze moved to where she was staring, and then darkened. It was at Luc Dinardi. He was chatting up the young trophy wife of an ageing banker, shamelessly flirting with her even though her husband was only a few metres away. Annoyance stabbed through him. He'd just warned her about Luc Dinardi, and here she was, staring at him.

'I told you—he'd eat you for breakfast,' he said tersely.

Her eyes dragged back to his. They seemed dazed. It annoyed Allesandro even more. 'Look, Luc Dinardi is not the kind of man your grandfather would let within ten metres of you!'

Laura just went on gazing, lips slightly parted, that dazed look in her eyes unchanged, quite ignoring whatever it was that Allesandro had just said. She was completely caught up in reliving that unbelievable, electrifying moment when that man— Luc Whatever—had come up to her.

He found me attractive! It was in his eyes! I wasn't imagining it! It was real—he really, really was eyeing me up! Me!

The balloon inside her that had been swelling with each sip of champagne, with each wonderful, miraculous moment that had passed since she'd walked in here, lifted off, filling her with exhilaration.

She didn't know how the miracle had happened—but it had. And that it was a miracle she was in no doubt. It was like being someone else—someone completely, absolutely different from the person she was. A magic door had opened, and she had stepped through into a glittering world beyond. A world that had always been barred to her.

But to which she now belonged.

Bliss and wonder speared through her.

At her side, Allesandro was saying something again. Sharp and annoyed. She didn't pay any attention. She wanted to go on revelling in gazing at the first man who had ever, in all her life, looked on her with desire...

Even as she gazed his eyes took time out from openly flirting with that Italian woman with the red dress and big hair and darted briefly towards her. There was a glint in them that made her breath catch. Then, a moment later, he was taking leave of the other woman and heading towards her. The glint in his eye was even more pronounced now. As he approached, he helped himself to two glasses of champagne, and proffered one to Laura.

'Your glass needs refreshing,' he murmured. He took no notice of Allesandro, all his attention on Laura, and she felt exhilaration and excitement flare in her eyes again. His appreciation was open.

'Luc—' There was a warning note in Allesandro's voice.

The other man ignored him. He smiled invitingly at Laura.

'So, have you seen much of the Eternal City yet, Laura?' he murmured, again giving her name the Italian pronunciation that made it sound so much more exotic.

'Not yet,' she managed to say, her voice suddenly breathless. He smiled. A pleased smile.

'Well, in which case you must allow me the privilege of being the one who shows you the glories of Rome! By day, it is wonderful—but by night...' His eyes held hers. 'It is magical! Let me show you—and what better time than tonight?'

His smile deepened invitingly.

Allesandro had had enough.

'Luc,' he said pleasantly, and went on in Italian, 'I will tell you only once more—go hunting elsewhere, understand? Laura is with me.' He then added a coda which was less pleasant, and detailed the unfortunate physical injuries that would befall him were he to ignore this adjuration.

Luc's eyes went to his, still glinting, but with taunting humour this time, as he replied in the same tongue. 'Well, well—seeking to disprove that rumour about an intimate Viale-Vincenzo merger, I see. Farewell, Delia—ciao, Laura—and as for this mystery granddaughter of old Tomaso, she must remain a mystery. And conspicuously absent from your life, no? Still, with a woman as beautiful as Laura, what charms could compete?' Once more, Luc's eyes swept over the female at Allesandro's side.

Allesandro felt his teeth gritting. Yet at the same time he was vividly aware that this general misapprehension about Laura's identity was an advantage. Right now her presence at his side was serving—with supreme irony!—to give a reason why he was not available for marriage to Tomaso Viale's granddaughter, and at the same time, if at some point it emerged just who Laura Stowe was, his original plan would have worked as well. Brilliantly! No one, but no one, could ever throw any accusation against him for being the kind of man who would refuse to marry an ugly woman—or marry one solely for the commercial advantages she brought.

Tomaso's guns were spiked, whatever happened, and that was all he cared about.

That, and getting Laura away from Luc Dinardi—and all the other men eyeing her up for size. It was time to get her out of here.

But his timing was just out. There was a reduction in the level of conversation, a parting of guests, and their hostess was making her way into the vacated centre. Gathering all eyes, she launched into her pitch for her chosen charity.

As he waited with mounting impatience for the speech to end, Allesandro could see Laura at his side, despite the two warnings he'd now given her, occupying her time in looking across at Luc again. Worse, Luc was smiling back at her.

Gritting his teeth, Allesandro counted the minutes till Christa Bellini was finally done, and there was a general movement of people. His hand closed over Laura's elbow.

'We're going,' he said tersely.

He steered her towards the doors, pausing only to deposit the glasses and murmur his farewell to his hostess, promising a sizeable donation to her charity, before heading back out into the mezzanine lobby, towards the bank of lifts.

'What's happening?' demanded Laura, disengaging herself from his grip on her elbow. She felt disorientated and confused.

'I'm hungry,' announced Allesandro. 'We'll dine here. There's a rooftop restaurant.'

Laura stared at him. 'What—just you and me?'

Allesandro lifted an eyebrow. 'You have a problem with that?'

'Of course I do! I don't want to have dinner with you.'

'You'd rather be tête-à-tête with Luc Dinardi?' he enquired caustically.

'Yes, actually.'

'Did I hear my name?'

Allesandro turned curtly. Luc Dinardi was strolling out of the function room, and in his wake were a bevy of other people in the same age group, one of whom, a very pretty blonde in a jazzy designer number, came up to Laura.

'Hi!' she said, with a warm smile, speaking English. 'I didn't get a chance to meet you yet. We're all going off for something to eat—do come!' She slipped a hand through Laura's arm. 'You've got to tell me who designed your dress. It's stunning!'

'I've no idea, I'm afraid,' said Laura. 'I don't know anything about fashion designers.'

The other girl gave a trill of laughter, as if Laura couldn't possibly be serious. 'I'm Stephanie, by the way, and this is Maria, and Gianni, and Pietro, and Lizzetta. Luc says he knows you already—but then Luc always knows all the most beautiful women! Just like Allesandro. Anyway, do come! We're going to this fantastic place that you'll adore, and then we'll go clubbing. Do you know Rome well?'

'I've never been here before,' admitted Laura.

Stephanie exclaimed in amazement.

'Oh, we'll show you everything—all the coolest places. Stick with us and don't worry! OK, everyone—let's go!' She switched to rapid Italian and set off, drawing Laura with her.

A heavy hand on her shoulder stayed her.

'*Momento*,' said Allesandro grimly. 'We happen to have a dinner reservation upstairs.'

Stephanie waved a hand dismissively. 'Oh, Sandro, don't be stuffy! Laura doesn't want to eat there—it's a totally draggy place! Come on, let's go!'

Laura was swept away. She couldn't stop it.

And she didn't want to.

It was the magic door again, opening to a world she had never been part of. Never been invited into.

But she was being invited there now.

As if she belonged to it…

CHAPTER NINE

FOR Laura, the next few hours passed in a whirl—a magical, delicious whirl—like being in a candyfloss machine. Young, rich, beautiful Italians, enjoying themselves expensively in Rome—and she was part of it. One of them. One of the beautiful people. For the first time in her life all Laura had to do was simply go with the flow, which took her with it into a heady, magical place.

She ate, she drank, she smiled—she danced. She didn't know where they'd gone, but it had flashing lights and a lot of music, and it was the kind of place that only some people got into. And she was one of them. One of the chosen ones who moved like gilded beings—beautiful people.

She gave herself to it. Laughing, chattering, dancing—all washed down with champagne. When they got to the club, more people joined them, and there were more introductions. She didn't have to say much, and wasn't capable of it anyway—it was enough, oh much, much more than enough, simply to be part of it. One of them. Belonging to this world. This beautiful world with beautiful people...

It wasn't real. She knew that—knew it somewhere very deep inside, very hidden. Knew it was only an illusion, a dream. A magic world that had temporarily opened its gates to her, and let her in. But she wouldn't think of that—wouldn't think of anything. Would only sit there, hair smooth and glossy, cascading round her face, her eyes huge with make-up, her mouth scarlet with lipstick, a glass of champagne always in her fingers. Included. Accepted.

Admired.

She could see it—see it in the eyes of the men there—how they acknowledged it in the way they looked at her. Smiled at her. Danced with her.

It was headier than champagne, more intoxicating than wine. Wonderful. Magical. Unbelievable.

Blissful.

Across the table she could see Luc Dinardi. He was flirting quite outrageously with Stephanie, who was responding in kind, but every now and then he would glance in Laura's direction, throwing an amused, wicked glance at her. She could not help but respond. She knew exactly what kind of man he was—the kind of man who simply flirted with and flattered all women—but never, of course, had she been included in that number. And now she was. For the zillionth time blissful disbelief washed through her as she glanced down the table at him, to catch his eye yet again.

He never did more than throw her looks, however, and she knew why. The reason was at her side—always beside her—all evening, like a dark, glowering presence. A black cloud at the edge of the brilliant, incandescent sunshine she was bathed in, a black cloud that she simply ignored. Defiance spiked through her. Why should she care if Allesandro di Vincenzo was his usual disapproving self? He'd made his reaction to her clear as a bell from the very first moment he'd ever laid eyes on her. Nothing pleased the man, did it? He'd disapproved of her when she'd looked awful, and he disapproved of her now! Well, so what? Anyway, it was his fault that she was here—she hadn't asked for it, hadn't asked for it at all…

But it had happened, all the same—like a miracle. And she would not reject it—could not for the life of her!—and if Allesandro di Vincenzo didn't like it…well, tough. He'd been one of the beautiful people all his handsome life—but for her it was a party she'd never been allowed in to before.

And she would revel in it while she could.

So she deliberately ignored him, setting him aside out of her consciousness, whilst she laughed and chattered about nothing, taking it in turns to dance with the men in their party.

Even, eventually, with Luc Dinardi.

It was a fast number, as they all had been, and she took to it unselfconsciously just like everyone else, feeling the heavy pulse go right through her, with the strobing lights and close proximity of all the other dancers. Then the track ended, and suddenly the whole mood of the place changed—the lights ceasing to strobe but now sweeping in slow arcs, the next track suffused with husked, languid tones.

All over the crowded dance floor couples were closing in on each other.

And Luc Dinardi was closing in on her.

His hands slid around her waist, drawing her to him, and he murmured something she could not hear, smiling into her eyes with clear, satisfied intent.

And then he was being removed.

'My turn,' said Allesandro, and took over, his hands sliding around her waist, serving to turn her away from Luc, remove him from her vision.

She could say nothing. The breath had suddenly left her lungs. As if of their own free will her hands slowly came up to rest on his shoulders. Her eyes met his.

In the dim light she could not make them out. They were dark, that was all, and the planed face was silhouetted by the slow sweep of the lights.

He began to dance with her, moving her like an inert puppet while she gazed up into his face.

Her breath was still stopped. So was her pulse. She could not feel it at all, and then suddenly it was there. Slugging in slow, heavy beats, making the breathlessness tighter yet. She could feel his hands on her hips, warm through the material of her dress. Feel the smooth surface of his dinner jacket beneath the polished tips of her nails. The plaintive sound of the singer wound through her head, mesmerising her senses.

His eyes held her. Winding around her, winding her to him, dark and fathomless. She gazed up into them, lips parted.

The pulse in her veins intensified.

How long they danced she had no idea. But eventually the singer reached the anguished end of his lament and the music changed tempo again. Allesandro led her off the dance floor.

But not back to their table.

'Time to leave. It's late, and I have to work tomorrow.'

Automatically, Laura felt herself resist.

'So go,' she said. 'I'm fine here.'

A derisive noise came from him. 'Luc Dinardi has plans for you. The only reason he's kept his distance is because of me. He was already pushing his luck moving in on you back there on the dance floor.'

Laura frowned. 'He's with Stephanie.'

Allesandro continued to steer her towards the exit. 'He and Stephanie are long-time exes. They hang out together when it's convenient, like tonight. She won't cramp his style, believe me.'

He reached the doors and guided her out. She shivered as the chill of the night air hit her after the heat of the club. She looked around. They seemed to be in some kind of side street, but she had absolutely no idea where they were in the city.

'My bag!' she exclaimed suddenly, realising she had left her evening purse on the table inside.

Silently, Allesandro reached inside his jacket pocket and handed it to her. Then he proceeded to slip the jacket from him and drape it around her shoulders. The warmth of his body heat eased through her, banishing the chill.

'Thank you—but won't you be cold?' Her voice was staccato. She felt disorientated, dislocated.

'I'm fine. Can you walk in those heels? There won't be any taxis along here.'

He started to walk down the narrow street. Laura walked beside him, one hand holding her evening bag, the other the lapels of his jacket, draped around her. She looked about her. The houses were mostly old, and tall, and the roadway, she noticed, was cobbled. Further down the road opened into another, slightly wider street. As they gained it, however, and she looked around, her breath caught.

There was a blaze of iridescent light coming from a little way further on, and as she focussed on its source she gave a little cry.

'It's the Trevi Fountain! Oh, please—can I see it?'

Allesandro glanced down at her. Her face was alight.

But then, it had been alight all evening—ever since that airhead Stephanie had scooped her up and set her up for Luc to rile the hell out of him by registering his obvious intentions. Well, he'd had enough—enough of running interference and standing guard over her. He'd gone along with it because—well, because she'd so obviously wanted to go, to be a completely different female from the one she'd always been.

And she'd succeeded. The stab of disbelief came again as he looked at her now. She'd spent the hours in the restaurant and then the nightclub being a totally different person from the one he knew. One he simply wouldn't have recognised. And it hadn't just been her looks—it had been her whole personality. Smiling, chatting, laughing, dancing, flirting…

His eyes darkened again. Oh, she'd been flirting, all right! Despite his warning he'd seen her glance down the table, meet Luc's eye as he looked her way, seen her register her awareness of him, her interest in him.

And she'd been perfectly happy to dance with him like that, right at the end, up close and personal with Luc Dinardi!

No wonder he'd had to take action and cut in on them! He'd had no choice. But dancing with her had been a mistake. A bad one. One he had absolutely no intention of remembering. Instead, to stop himself, he nodded.

'If you want. It's overrated, though. Most tourists find it much smaller than they expected. Not the fountain itself, but the square.'

But Laura didn't care. She hurried forward, as fast as she could in the high heels, with the long skirt of her dress clinging around her legs, still clutching Allesandro's jacket around her shoulders against the chill night air. As she gained the entrance to the little square her eyes went straight to the fantastic wall of sculpture and water that spouted and cascaded into the ornate pool of the fountain, lit from underneath so that the pool and gushing water were iridescent with light.

Even at this late hour there were hordes of people still present, crowding around the fountain's edge, backing up the steps behind. It was a small space, it was true, but Laura's eyes were only on the baroque splendour of the fountain. She paused, eyes wide, lips parted.

'It's fantastic!' she breathed. She half turned to Allesandro, standing beside her. 'I don't know anything about it—just that it's famous. And you have to throw a coin in it, of course.'

'Backwards, over your shoulder,' said Allesandro. He slid his hand into his trouser pocket and drew out some loose change. 'We'll need to get closer,' he went on, and started to usher her forward, threading through the throng as those who had had enough moved away. Eventually they were right by the lip of the fountain's pool. Laura trailed her fingers in the water, which seemed to glow with light.

'Here you are,' said Allesandro. He handed her a one-euro piece. 'Turn around.'

She did so, taking the coin and turning until she was facing away from the fountain.

'Will I hit anyone?' she asked.

'All clear,' he replied.

She flipped the coin over her shoulder. 'Did it go in?' she asked, as she turned back.

'Absolutely,' said Allesandro. 'It's that coin there,' he pointed to one of the mass of coins that lay in the bottom of the water.

'What happens to all the coins?'

'They get collected for charity, I assume,' he answered. He looked around him. 'God knows when I was last here doing this,' he mused.

'I'm sorry,' said Laura. She was suddenly awkward. 'You must think it really naff.'

He glanced at her. There was a stiff look on her face. It made her instantly recognisable as the Laura Stowe he was used to. Hostile. Prickly.

He gave a slight shrug. 'It's a tradition. And so,' he went on, his tone changing, 'is eating an ice cream afterwards.'

He nodded towards where a brightly lit gelataria on the far side of the square was doing a brisk trade. He led her across and they joined the queue. A polyglot of languages was all around them, and under the counter was a rainbow array of different flavoured ice creams. Allesandro translated.

'Melon sounds refreshing. But only a small one!' Laura said anxiously, glancing at the towering edifice the person ahead of them was being presented with.

Even with her request, the ice cream was still generously proportioned—as was Allesandro's.

'Coffee,' he said, as she looked enquiringly at it. 'Come on, let's get out of here.'

They made their way back outdoors again, Laura carefully starting on her ice cream lest it drip and run on her dress. She glanced at Allesandro. He was getting to work on his own ice cream, and as they headed along a quiet side street, away from the busy square, a sense of unreality came over her.

I'm eating ice cream with Allesandro di Vincenzo—and we've never had a civil word to say to each other!

It seemed bizarre—extraordinary—unreal. But then the whole evening had been unreal.

Magical.

And the magic was still going.

'Do you want to see the Spanish Steps while we're at it?'

His sudden question took her by surprise. She looked at him doubtfully.

'You said you had to be up early.'

He gave another of his shrugs. 'I just wanted out of that club. You said earlier you wanted to see Rome by night, so why not?'

She hadn't actually expressed any such desire, it had been Luc Dinardi, but she let it pass. She did want to see the Spanish Steps.

And she didn't want the night to end. Even if she had to be in Allesandro's company.

Not that he was being particularly irksome now. Nothing like, she realised, the person she was used to. He was being—well, nice. To her. It was amazing if she thought about it. So amazing that really the best thing was not to think about it.

Just to accept it. Accept the wonder of it as she was accepting the magic—the miracle that had happened to her tonight.

And part of that had to be wandering through Rome at midnight, in evening dress, one of the beautiful people...

With another of the beautiful people at her side.

A tiny shiver went through her—delicious, delightful. Amazed.

Her and Allesandro di Vincenzo...

Incredible! They were simply strolling along at a slow pace, steadily demolishing their ice creams, heading towards the busier street that Laura could see ahead of her.

'Can we walk there? To the Spanish Steps?' she asked.

He shook his head. 'It's too far—we'll take a taxi.'

When the ice creams were gone he requisitioned a cab and saw her inside. As he took his place beside her the taxi interior suddenly seemed a lot smaller. Instinctively, she squeezed to the far side, leaving the maximum gap between them. It was only a short ride, anyway, and without evening dress she could easily have walked the distance.

As she got out, she saw that the floodlit steps were just as thronged as the Trevi Fountain had been. She gazed past the odd-shaped fountain in the square at the base of the steps, up the ascent towards the twin-towered church and the obelisk at the top, while Allesandro paid off the cab.

'Keats died in a house here,' she said. 'That's all I know.'

'That one.' He nodded at a small, elegant edifice to the right of the steps. 'It's a museum now.'

'Why are they Spanish Steps?' she asked as she started to walk up them, lifting her long skirt as she did so. 'And why is the fountain that strange shape?'

Allesandro dredged his memory. 'On one side of the square,

here at the base, was the Spanish Embassy to the Vatican. The fountain is shaped like a boat because a boat was beached here after the Tiber flooded in the sixteenth century.'

'How many steps are there?'

He gave a laugh. It was an unexpected sound, and made Laura glance sideways at him.

She found her breath catching. She'd never seen him laugh, she realised. The most had been a civil smile to their hostess at the charity function earlier. But this—this was a laugh. Brief—but enough...

Enough, she realised, with a strange little hollowing inside her, to indent lines from his nose to the sides of his mouth, to lighten the planes of his face. Make him look—

Incredibly attractive....

Immediately she flicked her gaze away, lifting it upwards to look where they were climbing. No, she mustn't think about that. She really, really mustn't.

'I've no idea,' he told her. 'A lot more going up than down!'

She gave an answering laugh. 'Where does it go up to? What's that church?'

'The Trinità dei Monti—and no, I don't know any more than that. You'll need a guidebook.'

'What's that beyond the church?'

'It leads up to the Borghese Gardens—'

They gained the halfway point, where the steps opened up into a platform, and Laura paused, turning around to look back down over the steps, down over Rome spreading away beyond.

I'm half Italian, she thought. I belong as much here as I do in England.

But it didn't seem like that. She was only a tourist, passing through. The strange sense of dissociation she'd felt when Allesandro had whisked her out of the club assailed her again.

She gave a shiver.

'Are you cold?' An arm slid over her shoulder.

Instinctively, automatically, she froze. A moment later the arm was gone.

'If you're ready, we'd better make a move.'

Allesandro's voice was terse. Abrupt.

Without speaking they went back down to the roadway at the base of the square, where he swiftly commandeered another taxi. Laura looked out of her window, making no attempt to say anything more. That brief—*very* brief!—moment of feeling at ease with Allesandro had vanished completely again. Now she felt tense, edgy.

It was probably reaction setting in after the most unbelievable evening of her life. She still felt weird, dissociated.

Restless.

She glanced down at her hands lying in her lap, clutching her evening purse, her long, painted nails curved over the satin material.

Hands that were completely alien to her. *Her* hands were rough, battered hands, toughened with manual labour, not soft and manicured like the hands she could see now, with their false fingernails and glistening varnish. In her mind's eye she saw the hands lying in her lap morph and change back into the hands they had always been.

Suddenly fear stabbed her. For tonight, out of nowhere, she'd become Cinderella—had gone to the ball. Never expected, never hoped for. Never even dreamt about—for what would ever have been the point of dreaming about something she could never have? Tormenting herself with what she could never be? Far better simply to accept what she had always been.

Except that tonight, this extraordinary, miraculous night, she had become someone completely, absolutely different from reality. Someone it had just been so, so wonderful to be!

But now it was over. The end. *Finito*.

Bleakly, she turned her head to stare out of the taxi windows as the streets of Rome passed her by.

All over.

The taxi drew up outside the hotel she'd left only a few hours earlier in a state of happy excitement. Now she was as flat and drained as a burst balloon. Stiffly, she got out of the car and walked inside the lobby. Allesandro was still with her—presumably he would see her dutifully to the reception desk and see she had her key. Then he would go. Escape. Back to his own life.

Was there a woman waiting for him? There was bound to be. Allesandro di Vincenzo could have the pick of any woman who caught his eye.

Like a bolt from the blue, it struck her.

You caught his eye!

The moment burned in her senses. When you were standing there, in the entrance to the bar, he was transfixed by you—and he didn't know who you were, so it was real—real that you caught his eye—just for being beautiful. Beautiful enough for him to look at...

Almost she stumbled, then recovered herself and kept walking. But in her head was the memory, that extraordinary, unbelievable memory, of watching, all unknowing, Allesandro looking at the woman in the reflection.

Her stomach hollowed. All evening she'd blanked it out, refused to think about it, focussed only and exclusively on what had been happening to her—on the growing, thrilling awareness that men were looking at her, liking what they saw, admiring what they saw.

Wanting what they saw.

Luc Dinardi had been blatant about it. She'd let him be, because it had fascinated her, enthralled her, to see a man as obviously philandering as he was singling her out. Flirting with her. It had been heady—exciting to let him do it.

Safe.

Where that word came from, she didn't know. But it was there, all the same. That was why she'd ignored Allesandro's dark and dire warnings about him. Because they'd been pointless. Unnecessary.

'Your key, *signorina*.'

The receptionist proffered a key that looked like a credit card. Laura surfaced, and stared at it blankly. She'd never seen a key like that—but then she'd never stayed in a hotel like this before.

'You swipe it through the lock,' said Allesandro, taking it from her. 'I'll show you.'

He headed at a swift stride towards the lift. Laura followed him. Absently, she wondered if the clothes she had been wearing before she'd been handed over to that spa place had been taken up to her room. She hoped so, or she'd be completely stuck.

She looked after Allesandro. There was tension in his shoulders, and she realised with a start that she still had his evening jacket around her own shoulders. As the lift doors opened she shrugged herself out of it and handed it to him as they stepped inside the lift. He took it, but didn't put it on, just slung it over his arm. The fingers of one hand drummed on the metalled wall of the lift.

His face was closed. Laura looked at him covertly.

The man who'd given her a coin to throw in the Trevi Fountain, who'd climbed up the Spanish Steps with her, had gone. Back again was the Allesandro di Vincenzo she knew and disliked—looking his usual ill-tempered, annoyed self, not wanting to be where he was. She gave a mental shrug. Out of nowhere a tiny pang went through her, but she shrugged it off. Allesandro di Vincenzo was simply babysitting her up to her room, the way he'd done all evening, then he'd be off, and he'd be gone.

And the evening would be over. Finally over.

Again, that stab of emotion went through her. But what could she do about it? Midnight had sounded, and she was heading back from the ball.

She glanced at herself in the metalled wall. Like the walls in the bar, it acted as a reflecting surface, bronzed and muted. She stared at herself, wanting to remember this last moment of her evening.

As her eyes worked over her image, a sense of wonder suffused her all over again. It was miraculous, just miraculous! There was just no other word for it! She'd had all evening to get used to it, to catch herself in mirrors, or in the mirror of men's eyes, but this was the last time she would see it. She let herself gaze, taking in the beautiful lines of the gown that sculpted her body like a statue, the rich fall of her hair, and above all the dramatic beauty of her face…

And then, as she gazed at herself—helplessly, consumingly—as the lift swept upwards, she became aware that someone else was looking at her too. Someone whose eyes were narrowed, with a focus in them, with an intent, that made the breath dry in her throat.

Her eyes in her reflection went to his.

To Allesandro.

Everything stopped.

Just stopped…

There was no movement, no sound. Nothing except their eyes meeting.

Her stomach hollowed.

She was aware of everything, absolutely everything about him, in the minutest detail. The way his white shirt fitted like a glove over his lean torso. The way his fingers were splayed against the wall, where the drumming had ceased now. The way his sable hair framed the planes of his face.

The way he was watching her.

The blood began to slug heavily, around her veins. Something very deep inside her began to surface. Powerful, ineluctable, consuming.

Slowly, very slowly, she turned towards him.

The air was thick as muffled silk. The space they were in enclosed them. A world apart.

She met his eyes again. Not in reflection now, but in reality.

A reality that was drowning through her, thickening the breath in her lungs, the blood in her veins, the heavy pulse of her heart in her chest. She could see everything, everything about him, in total, super-focus.

As if a veil had dropped.

His image burned on her retina—the image he had burnt on it the first time she had set eyes on him, that had reburned itself every time she saw him again. She'd seen, but would not look. Would not. Because what would have been the point? A female like her, looking at a man like him…

She had refused to look at him—refused to pay him the slightest attention. Blanked him out and blocked him out. Fielded him out of her consciousness. Denying him access to it, denying her awareness of him.

No more.

Because he was there—right there—a hand's reach away from her in this breathless enclosed space.

The minute shudder of the lift, the silent slicing open of the doors, jarred her. Shocked her. For a second she just stood there, paralysed, and then she was moving out—moving on rapid, urgent footsteps. She didn't even know which way she was going. There was a long corridor ahead of her, and she started striding along it, as fast as her long skirts would allow.

'Laura!' The voice halting her was terse. Brusque. She turned.

Allesandro was holding her key. 'Your room is in the other direction,' he said.

With a breath, she plunged back past him, heading in the direction he'd indicated.

'Stop—it's this one,' his voice commanded from behind.

She halted, facing the door. Her heart-rate had increased. She wanted to be inside. Wanted it with an urgency that was like a pressure on her spine. She watched him slice the key through the lock, saw the light go green, and then she was pushing the door open, groping for the light switch.

He stepped inside, setting the key card into a socket by the door and then flicking a switch. Immediately the lights beside the bed came on, pooling the room with soft light. He glanced at her.

'Before I go,' he said, and his voice was terse, tighter than ever, 'I want to ensure you understand something.'

She stood stiff, wary—horribly aware, but denying it, refusing it, the way she always had. Always must. Because she had to—just...had to.

His dark eyes rested on her. They were expressionless, unreadable.

'Steer clear of Luc Dinardi. Do you understand? You're completely incapable of dealing with a man like that.'

His voice was a flat, brusque command. It made Laura flare in retaliation. Her nerves had been on edge, on the blade of a knife, infinitesimally balanced. Now the blade flashed out of nowhere. She couldn't stop herself.

'I don't need you to tell me that!'

The dark eyes flashed back at her. Like lightning. '*Dio*, you're a walking fire hazard! Tinder-dry! And, believe me, Luc would revel in striking the first match!'

'I'm perfectly safe from him!' she shot back. The blood leapt in her heart, flaring in her veins.

'You're not safe from yourself! Do you want me to prove it? *Do* you?'

He snaked out a hand, closing it over her wrist. It was like a steel band.

'Let me go!'

There was a glitter in his eyes now.

'Do you want me to?'

His voice had changed. Changed totally. Something had come into it that fused the vertebrae in her spine. A low, intent note.

'Do you want me to?' he said again, and at her wrist she could feel the iron band of his fingers, and then, like a whisper, the softest movement of his thumb against the delicate skin over the veins.

It was happening again. That thickening of the air. The thickening of the breath in her lungs, the slowing of the blood through her heart—everything slowing down. The world had gone into slow motion.

Slow motion as she dropped her eyes to her clasped wrist, and then lifted them again to meet his. Eyes that were no longer expressionless...

Eyes that were completely, absolutely, focussed on hers...

She heard the slither of his jacket to the floor, saw the half-open door press closed as he leant back, the movement drawing her forward. Towards him.

He said something in Italian. Low and urgent. And then her wrist was being bent back around her waist, the hollow of her spine was indented forward, and his other hand was there, on the fine, taut material of her dress, splaying out its fingers. She could feel each indentation. Feel the heat of his hand against her back.

It was exquisite, incredible. A sensation she had never experienced, never known.

Her lips parted. He loosed her wrist, using the fingers of his hand to graze lightly, so lightly, over her bared back.

He was caging her. She could feel his breath on her cheek, catch the tang of aftershave, see the dark glitter in his eyes. That absolute focus. Absolute tension.

Absolute control.

And still the exquisite grazing of her back played on her nerve-ends, dissolving each and every one of them...

Her hands—hanging loosely, limply at her side—started to lift. Of their own accord entirely the palms pressed against his torso. It was warm, the fine layer of cotton yielding to the hard wall beneath. She stretched her fingers wide, feeling the ridged smoothness of muscle flexing to her touch.

As if she were having on him the exact effect his touch had on her. A little breath parted her lips as she made that realisation.

Her breathing quickened, and she gave an intake of breath. Something fired deep inside her—something she had never experienced, scarcely even imagined, except perhaps as a teenager, watching a romantic movie when the hero swept the heroine into a clinch.

That sense of breathlessness, of wonder...excitement...intensified now, in the heady rush of reality, a thousandfold.

He said something. It was in Italian. She couldn't understand it. Didn't care. Didn't care about anything at all except feeling the brand of his hand on her back, the wall of his body beneath her hands, drowning into those beautiful long-lashed, dilated eyes.

His hands stopped moving. Pressed suddenly, splayed on her back.

Stilling her. Holding her.

Holding her ready for him.

His mouth came down on hers.

CHAPTER TEN

HER mouth was like velvet. Soft, so soft. She didn't know how to kiss him, but he didn't care. He knew how to kiss her.

Knew that he had wanted to all evening. Ever since he'd laid speculative eyes on the eye-catching woman with the show-stopping figure. She'd hooked his attention then and had gone on hooking it. Even through the seismic shock of his realising just who that fantastic body belonged to.

Oh, he'd tried to crush down that initial reaction—had worked at it all evening, telling himself, firmly and repeatedly, that what his libido wanted to do was totally and absolutely out of order. That this was Tomaso's granddaughter—and therefore firmly, very firmly, out of bounds! He had even told himself that even though she looked like a knock-out on the outside, on the inside she was stubborn, recalcitrant, uncooperative Laura Stowe, with her total charm bypass...

But the trouble was, he could tell himself that all he liked—but it didn't make a gram of difference! It was impossible, quite impossible, to think of her as Laura Stowe—impossible to merge her into the woman he had set out with from Tomaso's villa only that morning...

She was now someone quite, quite different.

Even her personality was different.

She was smiling, chatty, flirtatious.

Flirtatious! Yes—and with, of all men, Luc Dinardi!

Dio, he'd spent all evening silently grinding his teeth, watching her make eyes at the man—and then he'd had to physically unglue her from him on the dance floor. Only then had he finally got what he knew he'd wanted all evening—got her away from Luc and to himself! He hadn't even minded that she'd wanted to go and gawp at the Trevi Fountain, do the hackneyed tourist trick of throwing a coin in. He'd even found he was happy to indulge her, and had thrown in eating an ice cream with her as a bonus!

It had been an opportunity to prolong the time he had with her—to allow his eyes to feast on her, to enjoy that spectacular body of hers, sheathed in that breathtaking gown, to relish the stunning transformation of the whole incredible package of her even though he *knew* that, despite the amazing image she presented, she was still, underneath it all, Laura Stowe….Tomaso's granddaughter.

And that was exactly why he'd called time on their little midnight meander through Rome. Why he'd walked her briskly back down the Spanish Steps, into the first taxi available, and conducted her safely back to the hotel. Escorting her to the desk was only courteous—only what anyone would have done. But he had found that, given the slightest, *slightest* opportunity to delay, even by a few more minutes, the moment when he'd have to walk away from her, he'd grabbed it without hesitation, telling her he'd show her how her room key worked.

A fatal moment of weakness….

Disastrous—quite disastrous!

Because suddenly, devastatingly, the stubborn, uncooperative woman he knew, whom he'd had to bribe to get out to Italy, and who was the *last* woman on earth he wanted anything to do with, had changed everything. In the closed, confining space of the elevator she had gazed at her incredible reflection in the mirrored wall as if she still, after all these hours, could not believe what she saw. And then fatally, disastrously, her gaze had shifted…

In that moment the world had stopped, narrowed down into

nothing except that shimmering gaze in his reflected eyes, beamed back like a laser with a single, searing message.

Dio, he'd been completely unable to block it—to resist meeting it, answering it….

Oh, he'd tried! He'd tried—

But when the lift doors had finally opened, after what seemed like a timeless eternity, all the defences Allesandro had been deliberately and doggedly piling up between them had been ripped away like tissue paper. He had planned to leave her alone—except she'd already demonstrated she was a complete push-over for a slick-smooth operator like Dinardi, so he had decided to warn her, just one more time.

And what had she done? Thrown his warning back in his face yet again! And that had been it! Something had snapped inside him. Something that had been tense as a board all evening, ever since the bomb had exploded, and he'd realised that the woman who had turned his head was Laura Stowe.

Something had started to heat like molten metal in that searing, nakedly revealing exchange of eye contact just now—in that dangerously enclosed, intimate space…

And yet she was still defying him! Still bleating that she was safe…*safe*…with a body like hers, a face like hers, that would draw every wolf in town down on her to feast if they could. She bleated about how she was *safe* with the likes of Luc Dinardi.

So he would show her! *Dio*, he would show her! Show her just how *safe* it was to look the way she did!

It had been impossible to stop himself. Impossible not to seize her wrist, hold her just where he wanted to. Impossible not to challenge her. Test her. Prove her completely, absolutely wrong.

Because he had not been able to resist doing so.

Had not been able to resist closing them both into her bedroom, letting his hands do what they had wanted to do all evening—what he had fantasised about doing all evening—splaying across that dramatic, alluring expanse of bared skin which was just asking, *asking* to be touched.

That was all it had taken. He'd been lost. Incapable of pulling back. Incapable of holding to his pointless, impossible resolve not to do what he had wanted to do from the first moment of seeing her.

To hell with it! To hell with his noble resolve, his tedious, self-righteous denial, depriving himself of what every cell in his body was urging him to do.

And now he was doing it. Kissing her. Letting his mouth lower down over the lush, inviting velvet that had tantalised him with what it promised.

What he could promise her.

A new-made Venus, born of the foam, all untouched, just waiting, *waiting* to be brought to life, to be awakened to all that physical desire could bring.

He would wake her, touch by touch, kiss by kiss, caress by caress, bringing her to the consummation of her womanhood, newborn this night.

Slowly his lips moved on hers. She did not open to him, only stood, arrowed back against his holding hands, she splayed across her back in support, while her hands counterbalanced on him, the warmth of her palms imprinting through him. Slowly, slowly he teased her lips apart, feeling them quiver like the finest vibrato of a violin, and then, as his tongue eased within, he felt her give a soft gasp in her throat.

Wonder darted through him. This was a woman like no other! Every woman he had ever possessed had been experienced, skilful, sophisticated in the art of lovemaking. But the woman he held in his arms now felt amazement even at an intimate kiss.

As his kiss deepened he knew, with absolute resolve, that the journey he would take her on would pay searing tribute to the transformation he would make in her. And it would be a journey he would make with exquisite slowness, taking her with him every step of the way, at her own pace, showing her, step by step, just what it meant to be a woman.

Unconsciously, something shifted in his head. Oh, the desire for her was still there—intense, like an unquenchable fire—but something new had happened. Something that had slowed him, changed him.

He went on kissing her, each kiss a little deeper, a little more sensual than the last, letting her get used to it, letting her own response guide him. And she was responding all right. She was beginning not just to be kissed but to kiss him back. A sense of triumph eased through him. Her eyes had closed, and there was a strange, dreamy look on her face as he glimpsed her through half-dipped lashes. Again and again his mouth grazed hers, and found reply.

Excitement quickened in him. He wanted more—more than this—delicious though it was to feel her coming to life beneath his mouth.

Slowly, very slowly, even as he went on kissing her, he slid one hand down the expanse of her back, curving over the beautiful swell of her bottom. He resisted the temptation to linger there, and with a smooth, fluid movement, he had lifted her up, taking her weight across him, sweeping her into his arms.

Her eyes flew open, and he could see alarm in them, uncertainty. He drew back a little, seeking to calm her. He murmured soft words at her, unaware that he was saying them in Italian. But they seemed to soothe her, or something did, for as he dipped his head to kiss her once more, all the time carrying her towards the wide bed that waited for them, her face lit in a beatific smile.

It was like a bolt going through him. He gave a rasp in his throat, and then he was lowering her down, down upon the bed. He stood gazing down at her, pupils flaring. The dark indigo of her gown was tightly wound around her legs, outlining the column of each thigh, pulled tight across the vee between. The pull of the bodice around her breasts enrobed each one, rich and bountiful, for him.

She lay with her hands fallen back either side of her head, her hair like a burnished swathe across the pale expanse of the coverlet. She gazed up at him, eyes huge, lips parted, tenderly swollen from his kisses.

For a long, long moment he just looked down at her.

Meeting her gaze. Holding her eyes.

Then, as if at a silent signal, he began to strip the clothes from his body.

She watched him remove his clothes. Wordlessly, silently, methodically, swiftly. The tie went first—a ribbon of black slicked from his neck, dropped to the floor. Then he slipped the buttons of his shirt, working his way down the length of his torso with practised speed until a column of smooth, muscled flesh was revealed from neck to waist.

His cuffs went next, and he moved only to toss the links onto the bedside table in a fleeting flash of gold. Then he was shrugging off the shirt, letting it fall where it lay.

Her eyes widened. She could not help it. Her gaze was riveted to his chest—smooth, bronzed, lean, muscled. Like something from a poster in a teenage girl's bedroom.

But he was no poster. He was real.

Real—potent.

Wonder, incredulity seared through her, as it had done again and yet again from the moment that he had lowered his mouth to hers. She could not have stopped him if she'd tried. But she hadn't tried. Hadn't even made the faintest, frailest attempt to stop him.

It had been beyond her—quite, quite beyond her. Because she was beyond everything now—beyond everything she had ever known. She was in a new world even more miraculous, even more magical, than the one she had been taken into that evening, when the doors that had been shut to her all her life had been so wonderfully opened.

But this—oh, this was far, far beyond even that! This was fantasy made real—imagination made glorious, blissful flesh. Her eyes washed over him, taking in every sculpted plane, every honed, perfect outline of muscle, bone and sinew. He was just so *beautiful!* This breathtaking male beauty, perfection of form, a paean to masculinity.

She'd seen it once before, the image flashing before her eyes so briefly, when he'd stood, poised like a steeled arrow, by the edge of the pool. But she'd had to look away—terrified, aghast.

Ashamed.

Ashamed to be caught staring at such perfection when she...

But now! Dear God—now it was like a miracle! She could lie here, gazing up at him, rapt, captivated, and know that in his eyes would not be revulsion, or blankness, but something that melted every bone in her body.

Desire.

She quivered with the knowledge of it. It was like a glow in her, a radiance. He wanted her! Wanted her as a woman—a woman to desire, kiss, caress. Beautiful for him...

Beautiful to him...

She gazed up at him. He was naked now, and more than naked—aroused. But she was not shocked. His body was too perfect for that. How could there be anything shocking in so perfect a body? How could there be anything shocking in something so natural as desire?

She lifted her arms to him.

And he came down to her.

Slowly, very slowly, very carefully, he eased the fine dark indigo material of her gown from her shoulders. They had been veiled from him for far too long. The allure of the dress had been skilful—tantalising—revealing the long flow of her back but veiling from him what he now must see, must gaze on, must feast his eyes upon.

And more than his eyes.

She lay, gazing up at him, accepting everything that was happening. Her eyes were molten, hazed with desire. It hardened him even more. He'd had a sudden fleeting moment of consciousness that a fully aroused, fully naked male might be a sight too far for her—but she had simply lifted her arms to him, and at such invitation how could he have held back?

Now he was beyond holding back—far, far beyond. Now all his focus was on edging down the material of her gown, centimetre by centimetre, his fingertips grazing her flesh, circling with tiny movements as he eased her free and, exquisitely slowly, revealed her beauty to him. The cusp of her shoulder was bared, and then the fine sculpture of her collarbone, the hollow at her throat where he could not resist touching the languorous caress of his grazing fingertip to the pulse at her throat before resuming his task. At last the swell of her breasts was reached, curving beneath his gliding fingers as he edged—minutely, exquisitely—the material of the gown ever lower, until their whole lush beauty was bared.

He did not wait. Could not wait. He lowered his mouth to an already straining peak, enclosing it with his lips.

He felt it again—felt that low gasp in her throat. Lifted his head to see the flare in her eyes as he took her on the next, most exquisite step of her journey. He murmured again, words of reassurance, and then returned to her breast, his hands smoothing over the marble of her shoulders.

He moved from one breast to the other, laving, caressing, and slowly, inexorably, taking her with him to the plane of desire. He could feel her body responding, her breasts swelling and straining against his ministrations, and her response fired his. He wanted more—oh, much, much more.

His hands glided down, sweeping the last of the material from her arms, down over her waist, over her hips, lifting her briefly until finally he could add the rich material to the heap of his own discarded clothing on the floor.

And now she was nearly—so very, very nearly—ready for him. His breath caught. Desire pooled and hardened in him. She lay there, eyes molten, breasts peaked and bared, two tiny wisps of satin around her hips. One he dealt with instantly, slipping the fastening to her stockings and flicking the unwanted item to the floor, before turning back to glide each silken stocking from her.

But the other he took his time over. Setting his pace to one she could respond to.

He let his finger edge beneath the thin, flimsy satin that girdled the expanse of her hip, and then, deliberately holding her eyes, he let the heel of his hand palm her. She gave that quiver again—but no repulse, no shock.

Without moving his hand, propped on one elbow, he slowly lowered his mouth to hers and began to kiss her again. Now her mouth opened to him without hesitation, lavishing on him a sensual ardency that inflamed him. His heartbeat quickened in his chest, and it was with absolute control that he let his fingers indent into the scrap of material still veiling her from him and drag it downwards. Then it was gone, and he glided his hand back up the lustrous marble of her thigh to reach its goal.

With soft caresses he loosened her thighs, all the while his mouth twining with hers, and as his fingers eased to open her to him, touched the incredibly delicate tissues he sought, her kisses changed.

He felt the fire catch her. Felt it lick through her, quickening her.

It was all he needed. With absolute purpose he took her onwards, towards the ultimate intimacy he sought. She was moistening for him beneath his touch, and he felt her quiver with response, her arousal intensifying.

His own arousal was intense, almost unbearable. He craved his own satiation, craved the culmination of this journey he had embarked upon. But he must hold back—must ensure that she could come with him.

Already she was nearly there. As he drew back his mouth from her, he could see the glazed mist in her eyes that betokened her state of intense arousal. Her breath was quick, shallow, her nipples peaked and hard. Her stomach was taut, her fingers digging into the bedclothes, as if to slake the tension in her body.

But there was only one way to slake that tension, to release what his touch was building in her. He moved towards it, the pad of his thumb centering on the hidden swollen nub, moving in tiny circles, so minute…so powerful.

Her head arched back, her sight dimming. Soft, aroused… arousing…moans came from her throat. His fingers played loosely with the silken, dew-drenched folds, while his thumb continued its slow, relentless arousal.

He saw her release. Saw her breasts flush, her spine arch upwards towards him. Heard the cry in her throat, a gasp of wonder, felt the flux of her inner body pulse at his touch.

Instinctively, overpoweringly, he scooped her up to him, cradling her naked, ecstatic body in his arms, enclosing her in the safety of his embrace, clutched tight against him. His hand smoothed her hair, holding her head, while his other hand supported her arched back.

She clung to him, hands folding over his shoulders as if in desperation, until slowly, so very slowly, the tide ebbed away from her. She went limp in his arms, her eyes still unseeing. Gently he laid her back upon the bed. Softly he bent to kiss her mouth.

Her pupils came into focus, and she gazed up at him. She could not speak, he could see. He smoothed the hair from her damp brow.

Wonder swept over him. A woman, new made.

He kissed her again—softly.

Then not so softly.

With a groan, he pulled away from her.

'Momento—'

With an effort of will he had not known he possessed, he hauled himself off the bed, his eyes casting round. Then he saw it—his jacket crumpled by the door. He strode across, seized it, and plunged his hand into the inner pocket, pulling out his wallet and slicing into it.

Thank God! With gritted teeth he took out the silvered packet and returned to the bed.

She was still looking dazed—amazed. He gave a sudden grin down at her, filled with exuberance.

'Allesandro—' she whispered.

There was almost disbelief in her voice.

He dropped a kiss on her mouth, then lifted away. A moment later he was ready.

Time to make her ready...

She could still feel the slug of her heart, still feel the pulse of her body, still feel—gloriously, wondrously—the radiance of the glow that had consumed her, the bliss undreamt of, unimagined. She was floating—floating in an existence that was so wonderful, so beautiful, it was a transfiguration.

And yet for all its fire, all its wonder, she was not sated, was still rich with desire. Desire for Allesandro.

As he lowered himself to her, she opened her arms to him, cradling him, glorying in the feel of muscle and sinew of his back as she ran her hands along the length of him.

His body covered hers. His weight pressed her down. She could feel her breasts strain against him—feel her hips strain against him. And her eyes flared—feel the strong, hard length of his manhood pressing against her abdomen.

She wanted him. Wanted him with every fibre of her being. Wanted the strength of him pressing her down, filling her, possessing her. As of their own volition her thighs strained upwards, her hands indenting into the hollow of his back to hold him close against her. She wanted him—all of him—it was the entire focus of her being.

There was a restlessness growing in her. She could feel it. Her hands smoothed up and down his spine, hips and thighs pressing upwards. Yet he wasn't moving, wasn't answering her. She gazed up at him.

He was looking down at her—just looking.

But there was something in that look that shot a bolt of raw sexual excitement through her.

Then, slowly, with absolute control, he started to kiss her.

It was nothing like he had done before! Then, his kisses had been seductive, slow, sensual.

These kisses were urgent—hungering. He swooped on her mouth, plucking at it like a predator, his tongue twining with hers, fast and furious.

Excitement exploded within her. Her pulse soared, and every muscle in her body tensed unbearably. Her back was a bow against him, her thighs stretched, heels digging into the bedclothes. He was kissing her still, never ceasing, but now he was lifting his hips from her, his hand palming her breast, shooting raw pleasure through her. She gasped, deep in her throat, and his kissing deepened at the opportunity she afforded him. Then, abruptly, his hands had abandoned her. She felt bereft, filled with frustration for the loss of pleasure—but then, to her relief, new sensation detonated in its place.

He was parting her legs, sliding his hand between them to lift her hips to him, and then his fingers returned to her, to glide not with slow sensuousness, as before, but with swift, mounting urgency. His fingers slipped inside her. She gave a gasp, but it was swallowed by him, and then, before she could be conscious of what was happening, his fingers were gone—and in their place the long, strong shaft that was questing entrance, sliding into her with swift possession.

She cried out again, nails digging involuntarily into his spine. He was lifting his head to say something, but she could not focus, could only feel, like a spear inside her body, the possession that was like an abhorrence to her. Her hands snaked from his back to try and lever against his muscled chest, but he caught them, lifting them over her head, pressing them down.

'It will be all right! Wait—just wait!'

The panic in her eyes died. He held her eyes, held them imperatively, not moving, poised in time, and slowly, ineluctably, her muscles released their rejecting tension.

He kissed her eyes.

'It will be all right,' he said again, his voice low, intense. 'I promise you.'

Very slowly, very carefully, he began to move within her.

He watched her every moment. Holding her hands tight in his, fingers entwining with hers, he moved with slow, deliberate intent.

And with each slow, deliberate stroke her body started to change.

This was different. As different from the first sensual arousing, as the hungering urgency had been different.

This was possession. The possession of woman by man, of man by woman. Because she was possessing him just as much as he was possessing her. She was enclosing him, holding him captive in her body, releasing him only to let him stroke into her again, and yet again. A compelling, intimate pavane of taking and withdrawing, holding and releasing.

Each stroke building a fire that only one culmination could fulfil.

She could feel it start to happen. Feel the entire focus of her body on a place she had not even known existed. In her innermost core, reachable only by each slow, deliberate stroke. As her gaze held his, she could see that it was starting to happen. Just as she could see, from the darkening intensity in his eyes, that for him it was the same. Between them something flowed. Acknowledgement.

Acknowledgement of what was happening.

The world had ceased to exist. There was nothing. Nothing except their bodies, melded to each other.

Nothing except the fire building, stroke by stroke, within those bodies.

Focussing their entire beings only upon that fire.

Her breathing was harsh, laboured. Her throat tight and taut. Everything was focussed upon that one core place in her body, where the heat was building…building.

And then, like a sheet of white flame, it seared through her. Racing instantaneously to every cell in her body. Making her spine bow upwards, as if releasing an arrow. And in the same consuming moment he surged into her.

She gave a cry—unearthly, distorted—and it mingled with a shout from him, just as their bodies were crushing against each other, the fire sheeting through them both, so there was no difference between them, so that they burned as one body, one flesh. His strength bore her down, his hands gripping hers as her body bowed upwards to his.

On and on and on it went—the sheeting fire ripping her into another world, her mouth gasping for air as sensation took her body.

Until there was nothing left. Only exhaustion. Limpness. Muscles strained beyond endurance, body throbbing.

He collapsed down on her, as exhausted as she, panting as if he'd run a marathon.

She held him in her arms, cradling his exhausted, sweated body. He buried his face in her shoulder, and her hand smoothed the damp sheen on his hair. Heaviness weighed down on her. Not the heaviness of his body, but the heaviness of her own exhaustion. Her eyelids pressed down. Her hands stilled. Sleep, like a great drift, closed over her.

CHAPTER ELEVEN

IT WAS dark when she awoke. How much time had passed she did not know. The bedside lights were out. She opened her eyes, staring into the black velvet.

She was alone. Allesandro had gone.

She lay, heart full, trying to make sense of what she felt. Because she felt so *much*! Amazement, incredulity, disbelief—all were surging through her as she realised what had happened. She could feel it, not just in her mind, her memory, blazing like an incandescent light inside her head, but in her body too—a body that had changed for ever.

Wonderingly she let her hands drift down over her nakedness, as if they could feel the difference that had been wrought upon it. At the vee of her legs there was a tangible difference—something she'd never felt before—a dull, throbbing ache that had no pain in it, no pain at all. Simply—fulfilment.

That it should have happened at all! And with, of all the men in the world, Allesandro di Vincenzo!

Disbelief swept through her again, like a tide of incredulity.

She shut her eyes against the inky blackness and immediately, vividly, he was there again in her mind—his body as incredible naked as it was fully clothed.

He made love to me—Allesandro!

The incredulity ballooned, melded with a quite different emotion—one that made her feel light as air. Inside her head words formed.

This can never be taken from me. Never!
I will have this memory, this truth, for ever!

Wonder, delight and amazement filled her whole being, her face lighting in a smile that made her draw deep breath.

I never, ever dreamt that anything so wonderful could happen to me!

But then, the entire evening had been a wonder, a miracle…

As her eyelids grew heavy, and sleep fluttered down on her again, she found her lips moving in silent gratitude, and as she slept she still smiled, her body rich and replete—an outcast no longer.

Allesandro reached for his coffee cup and stared into its inky depths. He was standing in the formidably modern kitchen of his formidably modern apartment, and he was filled with self-disgust.

How could I have done it? How could I?

Disbelief warred with his self-disgust. But he could disbelieve all he liked—it did not alter the truth.

He had had sex with Laura Stowe.

And the knowledge made him sick to his stomach.

It was the ringing of the telephone beside her bed that finally woke Laura. She'd slept deeply all night, and now she was still groggy as she reached for the handset.

'Hello?'

'Laura! Hi—it's Stephanie! Do you want to meet for lunch?'

Laura blinked. 'Oh. Um—I—I don't know—'

She fell silent. Waking had brought consciousness, and consciousness had brought, like a douche of cold water, the realisation that the ball was over and she was Cinderella once more.

'Go on, do—I'm dying to take you shopping. I know these totally brilliant boutiques you'll never find on your own! Look, I'll be with you at one, and we can zoom off then. Must dash! *Ciao!*'

She'd rung off before Laura could say anything more.

Dismay pooled in Laura as she slowly replaced the receiver. Even more slowly she made herself get up, and out of bed, head for the *en suite* bathroom. With absolute dread she took a breath, and stared at herself in the mirror.

It would be grim. She knew it would be grim. All the magic from the night before would be gone. She knew it. Knew it with every cell in her body.

She blinked. There was something wrong with the mirror. There had to be. A reflection was staring back at her. A woman. A woman with a lush, voluptuous figure, tousled, wanton hair, and with the dark, smoky smudge of unremoved make-up still darkening and deepening her eyes beneath the arching wings of her eyebrows. She lifted her fingers to her mouth.

The magic was still there...

She moved her head slightly and the cloud of dark hair lifted, then settled again, still tousled, still beautiful.

Just like the rest of her...

Slowly, very slowly, she began to smile...

Allesandro had not slept. Now, with punishing self-control, he was dressing himself in clothes suitable for the office. He shouldn't, he knew. He was being a coward. He knew that too. The last place he should go now was his office.

But he just did not have the nerve to do what he knew he had to.

So instead he drove his entire staff as if he were the devil, with red-hot whips. It helped to stop him thinking.

Remembering.

But it made not the slightest difference. He was still filled with self-disgust.

How could I have done it? Warning her about Luc Dinardi with one breath and then doing exactly the same as him with the next. Seducing her! Taking her virginity!

It had been self-indulgence! Nothing more than that—total self-indulgence, without the slightest sense of responsibility or consideration. He had taken her simply because he'd wanted to! Yielded to an overpowering selfish urge! Sexual appetite—raw and irresponsible!

The girl had spent her life being less sexually attractive than a pair of old boots, and then suddenly, in a single evening, she had been transformed into…a siren! A knock-out! A stunner!

Of *course* she had been overwhelmed by it! Of *course* she hadn't had the faintest idea of the impact she was having on every male in eyeshot! She'd been like a kid in a candy store and hadn't had the faintest idea the candy could bite back! *Dio*, he'd spent the evening trying to protect her from the kind of male who would have taken everything she had no idea she was offering—and then what had he gone and done? He'd gone and helped *himself* to her! He was supposed to be guarding her! Not seducing her himself! She was Tomaso's *granddaughter*, and he'd taken his pleasure of her and helped himself to her virginity.

And so what—so *what* if taking Laura to bed had proved the most exciting encounter he'd ever had?

He shouldn't have done it! That was all there was to it. He'd taken selfish, ruthless advantage of a vulnerable woman whose own grandfather had entrusted her to his care! There was no excuse for him…

Into the self-condemnation fell another realisation, like a stone. *I'm no better than Stefano with her mother…*

For a moment, cold iced in his spine. Then, taking a deep intake of breath, he knew what he had to do. Had to face up to. With extreme reluctance he picked up the phone and contacted the hotel. No, she had not checked out. At least, not yet. He still had time to get to her—to apologise. Apologise for being no better than her own philandering father…

Grimly, he left the office, got into his car, and headed for the hotel, the question still burning in his brain. His self-disgust had not eased by an iota.

But it turned instantly into a completely different emotion as he walked into the hotel lobby.

Laura was there. His eyes went to her at once. With one part of his brain he registered her presence—her appearance. She was looking just as stunning as she had last night, though now she was wearing an eau-de-nil shift and a bolero jacket in a slightly darker shade, a pair of dark glasses pushing her lush tresses back off her face, her feet in low heels. She looked instantly glamorous and instantly show-stopping.

But with the remainder of his brain he registered something that made fury slice through him and wipe everything else from his consciousness.

She was standing talking and laughing to Luc Dinardi, who was standing far, far too close to her, with that vacuous airhead Stephanie hanging beside them. Immediately Allesandro's eyes darkened. He strode forward.

Laura saw him immediately. And as she saw him her face lit. As if the sun had come out inside her.

Allesandro felt himself reel.

Dio, it was as if she was *pleased* to see him! As if he hadn't been like a libertine and Lothario to her the night before. Taking his pleasure with her and then abandoning her!

'Sandro—*ciao*. I was just taking the girls off for lunch. Won't you join us?'

Luc's *uber*smooth voice would have melted butter. Allesandro threw him a dagger look. Had it been steel, it would have slayed him on the spot. He went up to Laura, his hand closing over her elbow with automatic possession.

'No,' he said, with more curtness than social nicety warranted. 'And neither can Laura. We're running late already—Laura?'

She had time only to smile with confused apology at Stephanie and Luc, and wave goodbye, before Allesandro strode off with her.

'Can't they come with us?' she asked, conscious of having just waltzed off when they'd come to the hotel to see her.

'No,' said Allesandro. His voice was even more curt. 'They wouldn't like the place I've booked. Not their style.'

'Oh,' said Laura. But more than that she couldn't speak.

The same emotion that had lit her up inside as Allesandro had walked up to her was making it impossible to say anything more. Impossible to do anything except be handed into the car waiting for them in the hotel portico, be swept off into the monstrous Roman traffic.

There seemed to be a glow inside her, a buzz—like a hive of bees.

Allesandro settled himself back in the car, then looked across at her. For one long, long moment he held her eyes. Laura let him—let him look at her.

She looked good again, she knew. When she'd got up after Stephanie's call, she'd discovered—as she'd been in no state to do the night before—that as well as her own ancient suitcase that she'd brought from England, another one had been left on the luggage rack in the room. It was an expensive suitcase, and inside, when she'd opened it wonderingly, were clothes.

Clothes every bit as gorgeous as the dress she'd worn last night. The health spa place must have supplied them, along with the evening outfit. She looked through them, thrilled at them, every one a designer number. In the end she'd chosen the outfit she had on now, then spent time experimenting with the lavish contents of the third item left in her room—a huge vanity case stuffed to the brim with creams and cosmetics.

And her experiments, uncertain though they'd been, had worked! She had seen the proof of it as Allesandro had walked up to her—and now, again, as she let herself be bathed in his regard.

'It's like magic, isn't it?' she said. There was wonder in her voice, and still a shred of disbelief.

He nodded, slowly. Then, in a halting voice, he said, 'About last night—'

She leant across. Cupped a hand around his chin, feeling the touch of his skin beneath her fingertips. Lightly, instinctively, she kissed him.

Then, with two simple words, she made it all right for him. And for her.

'Thank you,' she said.

They lunched in a restaurant in the Tramontine area of Rome, across the Tiber. It was full of tourists, with its twisting old-fashioned streets and piazzas, but Laura loved it. And she loved their lunch of huge bowls of spaghetti in tomato sauce, washed down with table wine.

There was no one there that Allesandro knew, and he was glad of it.

He wanted Laura all to himself.

As she coiled a thick rope of spaghetti around her fork, he heard himself saying, 'I can't believe I thought you were fat.'

She looked across at him. There was a look on her face that was, he registered, of all things, mischievous. Laura Stowe—*mischievous!*

'I'll probably run to fat, though. But till then I'll make the most of it.'

Make the most of it...

The words seemed to echo in the air between them.

But they said nothing, neither of them. Instead Allesandro told her about Rome, and she listened avidly. After lunch they strolled around the Tramontine some more, and then Allesandro piled them both into a taxi and took her on a whistlestop tour of the city's most famous sites, from the Castello Sant' Angelo—'Tosca,' said Laura knowledgeably—to the infamous Coliseum— 'Built on the site of Nero's Golden House,' Allesandro informed her. She was fascinated by everything, and when, at the end, Allesandro asked her if she wanted to go to the opera that evening, her face lit with pleasure.

So he took her to the opera, and afterwards he took her back to the hotel—and to bed.

It was the obvious, the only thing to do.

And it was every bit as good, and incredibly more so, as it had been the night before.

This time he did not leave.

CHAPTER TWELVE

'THIS is just heavenly!'

Laura sighed pleasurably as she lifted her face into the sun, sitting at the breakfast table on the terrace of the old-fashioned de luxe hotel set high above the dramatic Amalfi coastline.

But then everything was heavenly! Absolutely everything. Everything in the entire wonderful, beautiful world!

And the most wonderful, beautiful, heavenly thing about it was sitting opposite her, wearing a pair of sunglasses that made him look so cool he must surely melt in the southern Italian sun that was blazing down on them from a cloudless spring sky.

A smile indented his mouth. His wonderful, beautiful, heavenly mouth...the mouth that went with the eyes, when he took those incredibly cool dark glasses off, and the sable hair that feathered in the lightest breeze lifting from a thermal coming up the cliff face, and the fantastic lithe body currently looking so breathtaking in an open-necked shirt with a light sweater draped with incomparable Italian elegance over his svelte shoulders...

'Where would you like to go today? Herculaneum?'

Laura shook her head regretfully. 'I ought to, I know, and perhaps one day I will. But Pompeii was so sad and terrible I don't think I can bear to see another destroyed city. It seems too dreadful that everyone had to die like that, and though I know the sites have yielded an invaluable amount of information about the Roman era, it was too high a price to pay for it.' She gave a little shiver that was nothing to do with the temperature of the air around them.

'Then how about Capri? Touristy—but it still has its charms, nevertheless.'

'If you can face it, I'd love to! But you really don't have to lug me around to all the tourist places, you know.'

His mouth quirked. 'It's an education for me. You know more about them than I do.' He nodded at the hefty guidebook that was lying on the table beside Laura's place.

She made a face. 'I like knowing things. But I appreciate it might be boring for others.'

'You mean airheads like me?' Allesandro quirked a good-humoured eyebrow.

Laura shrugged with a relaxed gesture. 'Not everyone likes history—it's not obligatory.'

'Maybe I just take it for granted. Italy has a surfeit of history, so we just get used to it being around the whole time.'

That might be true, thought Allesandro, but some things he just didn't get used to. Couldn't get used to.

Laura.

Laura Stowe.

Being here with her.

Even after nearly a week of being with her, he still felt disbelief and amazement wash over him. To be here with Laura Stowe, of all people. Tomaso's boot-faced, grouchy, stubborn-as-hell granddaughter! Except that—yet again he felt himself give a mental shake—she wasn't any of those things any more...

Not one.

It was as if her personality had changed as unbelievably as her appearance. She just was *not* the same person she had been! His veiled eyes studied her as she sat, gazing appreciatively out at the azure view beyond the terrace. It wasn't just that she was amazing to look at, wearing a deceptively casual outfit that didn't need a designer logo to show the credentials which were amply demonstrated by the favours it did her figure, she was just completely different to be with. Gone completely was the prickly, sullen, cussed Laura who'd used to infuriate him. The one who'd refused, point-blank, to show the slightest willingness to co-operate with him...

The new Laura—his eyes washed over her again automatically—was the most co-operative, easygoing, relaxed, accommodating woman he'd ever known! She revelled in everything—everything! From that day when he'd taken her off to get her away from Luc Dinardi she'd done nothing but radiate pleasure and wide-eyed wonder and enthusiastic delight—from the opera and post-theatre dinner to what had come after...

She'd sat through Verdi's *Don Carlos*, her expression rapt and her eyes wide, looking a knock out all over again in a silver-grey gown, just below knee length, that had hugged every line of her fantastic body, and she was fulsome in her gratitude to him for taking her. As for himself, he'd paid scandalously little attention to the music—he'd been all too burningly aware of her sitting beside him, of the scent of her perfume tantalising him almost as much as the shadowed outline of her body...

By the end of the evening he'd thrown caution, reticence, guilt—everything—to the wind! How could it possibly have been otherwise? He was flesh and blood, that was all—how could he possibly have not done what he had? Her entire reaction—completely unfazed, untraumatised, un-anything-negative at all!—to what had happened so unintentionally, so unforgivably, that first unbelievable night, when she'd been transformed into that 'other Laura' who was now her only reality, had made it impossible for him to resist her.

So he hadn't. That was all. And neither had she resisted. The absolute opposite! She had simply gone into his arms as if there was nothing in the slightest strange or bizarre about it! Let alone as if she'd been shocked or dismayed or appalled at what he'd done! As if she had never been that bolshy, uncooperative, deeply unattractive woman that she quite simply was not any more...

And with every day that passed it was more and more difficult to remember that she ever *had* been that 'other Laura' who had so infuriated and repelled him. She was growing dimmer and dimmer in comparison with the glowing, vibrant reality of the enticing, easygoing, fun-loving 'new Laura' as here with him now.

Why *was* she here with him? He didn't need to think much about that one. He'd whisked her off from Rome for two excellent reasons—to stop Luc Dinardi in his tracks, and simply because he wanted her to himself. It was a straightforward explanation for a straightforward situation. It didn't require huge psychological analysis, or brooding introspection. He had taken Laura to the Amalfi coast because he'd wanted to go—and so had she. Just as he'd taken her to bed because he'd wanted to—and so had she. End of story. Why ask questions about it? Why not just enjoy what was happening? He was—and so was she. They both were. They were having a simple, uncomplicated time together. Enjoying each other's company both by day and by night.

Especially by night.

Again, disbelief washed over him—even though it was milder now each time it hit him. How could the woman he spent these incredible nights with have anything at all to do with the female he'd known up till now? It was more than the incredible transformation in her appearance and her personality that made every night he spent with her so out of this world. It was something he'd never encountered before in any woman.

It was, he knew with a clarity that was impossible to deny, as if sex was a brand new invention and Laura had just discovered it. Which, of course, he mused, was exactly what she had done.

Discovered sex. Discovered how wonderful an experience it was—just as *he* was discovering just how incredible that made it for him in return. If anyone had ever told him that taking an inexperienced female to bed—let alone a virgin!—could be interesting, he'd have laughed. But he wasn't laughing now. And it was because of Laura—because she was just so *amazed* by the whole thing! So incredibly open and ardent! It wasn't about *what* they were doing together—it was about how they were doing it. How *she* was doing it. As if she were on the most incredible journey of her life—and he was taking her there, going with her, being with her. Every step of the way.

A smile of reminiscence for the night before played around his mouth. Her wonder, her amazement and pleasure—her open, wide-eyed pleasure—made each time with her like nothing he had ever experienced before. It was nothing to do with skills or sophistication—let alone copious practice!—with Laura it was something quite different—something very precious, something quite unique for him.

He got to his feet and held out a hand.

'OK, so Capri it is. Let's head down to the harbour and find the boat.'

He waited while she stood up and slid her hand into his. It was warm, and her fingers fitted between his. As they headed off it occurred to Allesandro that he had never walked along holding hands with a woman.

But he didn't want to think about that either. Right now, he wanted to show Capri to Laura. And her enjoyment of the day would be his too.

Laura sighed with sheer happiness and leant her head against Allesandro's shoulder. His arm was around her, and it was warm and secure against the bumping of the launch on the sea, heading back to the mainland in the early evening, with the sun setting behind her and the wind blowing the hair back off her face.

It had been another gorgeous day, and though, as Allesandro had warned, Capri was touristy, it had also managed to rise above its own popularity. They'd done all the touristy things— like taking the funicular railway up to Anacapri, high above the little town of Capri, and of course taking a boat into the famous Grotta Azzura—the Blue Grotto—as well as taking in some, but by no means all, of the plentiful classical ruins of the palaces favoured by Roman emperors. Allesandro had been amiable and good-natured about her desire to see as much as time would permit, and she had been warm in her thanks to him for it.

As ever, a sense of amazed wonder came over her. Not just

that she was here at all, in such company, but that Allesandro was just so…well, *nice*—it was the only word for it! He was easygoing and relaxed and fun and good-natured, quite simply a joy to be with.

And that was just by day…

By night—oh, by night he was beyond all her powers of description. She'd stopped trying to think about it. It was impossible! As impossible as all that had happened to her—was still happening! The door which had been closed to her all her life, locked and barred, keeping her out, had suddenly been flung open, and she had been swept through into an enchanted world. She was suddenly no longer the outcast, the outsider, the one who could never, ever join in.

And now she was here, one of them, and what greater proof could there be than the man who had his arm around her now? Because if he, Allesandro, could think her someone who belonged in the world to which he so obviously, so effortlessly, belonged, then she could have no doubts whatsoever.

He wanted her—he really, really wanted her! He had swept her off to bed, then swept her here, to the most potently romantic place in Italy, spending the days with her—the nights with her!—for no other reason than because—well, because he obviously *wanted* to.

He wanted to be with her—because why else would a man who looked like Allesandro di Vincenzo spend time with any woman? His looks were so spectacular—honed by his wealth and privileged lifestyle—that he could, she knew perfectly well, have had any woman he wanted. She had known that the first moment she'd laid eyes on him, looking—she gave a reminiscent smile—so impossibly out of place in the soggy Devon rain on her front doorstep. He was in a class of his own—the kind of man who would be surrounded by the most beautiful and glamorous women, and he could take his pick of them. So if he'd chosen her, and he had, then it was proof—absolute, incontrovertible proof—that she was indeed transformed.

Oh, this wouldn't last! How could it? Why should it? Men like

Allesandro drew women like flies! But it didn't matter that this was only temporary. All that mattered was that it was true—that it was really, really happening. That she was here with him because he wanted her. Desired her.

She leant against him, rejoicing in the strength of his chest, the tightening of his arm around her shoulder, the warmth of his body embracing hers in the wind billowing over them as the launch skimmed exhilaratingly over the sea's surface. The noise of the motor and the waves and wind made talking almost impossible, but she was content, oh, so much more than content!—to simply lean back against his lean, strong body and be happy, so very, very happy.

Because how could she be otherwise? How could she be anything but glowing with happiness, with sheer *joie de vivre*? Everything was wonderful, magical, fantastic! She was in love with life for the first time in her life. On a sudden impulse she lifted her head, craning her face towards him, and kissed him lightly, joyously, on the mouth. Not with passion, or sensuality, or desire, but just with sheer happiness.

'Thank you,' she said, her eyes glowing.

He gave his quirking smile, amusement in his eyes, and appreciation too. Then she relaxed back against him again and went back to simply enjoying the ride.

Happiness was rich within her.

CHAPTER THIRTEEN

'ALLESANDRO! No! Oh, my God—no. Don't!'

Allesandro lifted his head. 'You don't like it?' he asked, the look of wicked astonishment on his features barely visible in the dim light of the room.

He was answered by an expression of agonised self-restraint and barely suppressed laughter.

'You're doing it on purpose, aren't you?' Laura accused, as she laced a hand into his hair to hold him back from her. 'It's not fair!'

'Yes, but you see afterwards you make it up to me, no?' His eyes danced wickedly. As he spoke, his fingers started to weave a devastating trail where his lips had just been. 'So—still going to try and stop me?'

Laura's free hand snaked out and tried to grab his wrist, yank it away. But as her fingers closed around it he countered by suddenly rolling her over, so that she could only give a gasp, finding herself splayed across him.

'And your next move?' he invited.

Laughter sparked in her eyes as she levered herself back. Her breasts were full and engorged, her whole body rich and ripe, energised with an exhilaration that made her feel vibrantly, vividly alive. She ought to be tired—exhausted, even!—but she wasn't. She felt wonderful—absolutely wonderful. On an impulse, she wrapped her arms tight around the lean, muscled body that she knew so intimately now, and yet she was still so completely amazed by it—and by what it could do. Her hair fell like a cloud around them, and she rocked them both together gently for a moment in sheer happiness.

His arms came around her naked back and he returned her embrace. Then, returning to business, he moved, his hands to cradle her face and lift it smoothly but purposefully. 'It's no use,' he told her, with mock solemnity belied by the glinting gleam in his dark, long-lashed eyes, 'I shall have my wicked way with you—'

Her expression dissolved. 'Nothing that gorgeous could be wicked,' she said. Then, with an extravagant gesture, she flung herself off him and let her hands fall either side of her head on the pillow.

'Go on, then! I yield to my fate! Lord…' she gave a mocking sigh '…what I endure!'

His grin was like a wolf's before striking as he limbered up and moved to arch his body over her, and then, holding her eyes like a noose, he slowly, very slowly, very deliberately, slid himself down the bed. Elbows indenting into the sheet either side of her, he eased his hands along the smooth porcelain of her flanks, to come to rest on the cusps of her softly rounded hips.

'This,' he announced, and his voice was low and husked, with a timbre in it that made her bones quicken and her breath catch as slowly, exquisitely slowly, he lowered his head to her once more, 'may take some time.'

It did. It took a long, sweet, incredible, endless time, and by the time he was done she was as weak as a kitten, as spent as a candle melted into a pool of molten wax.

When, finally, he drew his body alongside hers and folded her into his arms like liquid, she was far, far beyond words. He held her, limp and boneless in his embrace, marvelling at the incredible intensity of her response, and more—at how she had accepted this most intimate of caressing with joy, with an open, natural pleasure that had made the experience as intense for him as it had been for her.

But not quite…

He gave her time—time that she needed to come back to

him—and then, as he felt her start to stir in his arms, he kissed her softly.

'And now,' he murmured pleasurably, 'it is time for the "afterwards" I mentioned, *no*?'

Laura's eyelids flickered a moment. Then she gave a yawn. A large, exaggerated yawn.

'Oh, I'm far, far too tired, darling…far too tired,' she drawled, in an equally exaggerated English accent. 'Another time, perhaps…'

She yawned again for good measure, then ruined it by opening one eye to see his reaction. He was grinning down at her.

'Nice try,' he said. Then, sliding his arms out from under her, he lay back beside her, calmly folding his arms down under his head and tilting his face towards her, his body displayed to her in all its masculine glory.

His dark eyes glinted.

'Take me,' he murmured. 'I'm yours.'

He closed his eyes and waited expectantly.

Laura snuggled up closer to him and started to let her fingers drift over the perfect musculature of his chest.

'Is this what you wanted?' she asked enquiringly.

'Uh-huh,' he answered, his eyes not opening.

She let her fingers trail a little lower, to outline each honed ab one by one.

'And this?'

'Uh-huh.'

She finished with the abs and moved on. She felt his whole body quiver in response to her caress.

'And this?' she murmured, her voice even lower, even more enquiring.

A sigh of deep, deep satisfaction exhaled from him.

'Definitely. Very, very definitely.'

'Oh, good,' she answered, and then it was her turn to slide her body down the length of his.

As for Allesandro—he lay back and thought of heaven. Which was exactly where Laura took him.

And afterwards he held her tight, so tight in his arms, until the fingers of the newly risen sun blazed into the room and he awoke to a new morning and another day with Laura.

How many days had passed? Was it four? Five? Six? Seven? Even more? He didn't know and he didn't care. He was, he knew, quite deliberately refusing to think about anything else. Anyone else.

Most of all he was refusing to think about Tomaso. And the fact that he was here with the old man's granddaughter.

His thoughts cut out. No, he wasn't about to let himself go down that route. He wasn't going to think about Tomaso, or his machinations, or anything to do with Viale-Vincenzo. He would continue to blank them out. Refuse to acknowledge their existence—refuse, right now, to acknowledge the existence of anything other than what he was doing at the moment. He was simply going to spend time here, with Laura, taking it day by day, night by night, and nothing else. Nothing else at all.

It was all he wanted.

And it was all Laura wanted too, it seemed. She seemed perfectly content just to stay in this self-contained cocoon, with him, being tourists by day and lovers by night, talking about nothing more than the sights and places they'd visited, or planned to visit, or about things like films and theatre and books and music. Nothing whatsoever about themselves, or their families, or anything at all that might, they both knew, lead them back to things neither of them wanted to think about. No, for both of them, he knew, the immediate present was all either of them wanted.

And it was a present without questions—questions about why they were here together—because questions needed answers, and answers were something Allesandro did not want to provide. And it seemed Laura did not either, for she neither said nor did anything whatsoever that asked or implied any question about just why or how they'd come to be lovers here—let alone what might come next.

All that came next was another day, as relaxed and enjoyable as every day had been—driving around, taking in the sights, wandering around resorts like Positano, or quieter more sedate towns in the hills like Ravello, having coffee, taking lunch, enjoying views, taking things easy, pleasantly, comfortably, unhurriedly. With nothing to do but enjoy themselves—and accept each day and night as it came. Shutting everything else out.

But eventually he could shut it out no longer. The phone, one morning, was insistent—and so was his PA on the other end of the line. When she spoke to him Allesandro realised why. Up till now he'd simply told her to put any business to the other directors. But now he knew he could not put off company affairs any longer.

'I'm sorry,' he told Laura, 'but I have to get back to Rome.'

As she got up and set about getting dressed, started to pack, she didn't make a fuss. She just got on with it. Accepting it. Not asking questions, either of him or herself.

They set off after breakfast, and all that Laura allowed herself was a single moment of simply drinking him in, outlined against the azure sea far below, as they sat eating breakfast on the sunlit terrace for the last time.

Remember this, was all she allowed herself to think.

And one other thing.

Just before they quit their room she suddenly put her hand on Allesandro's arm. He turned his head to look down at her.

'Allesandro, I just want to say thank you,' she said. 'For everything.'

Her eyes were wide and calm. Their message clear.

Then lightly, very lightly, she lifted her face to his and brushed his mouth, like a butterfly's wing.

Then she walked out and set off down the corridor to the lift.

They talked very little on the journey back to Rome. Laura knew why. There was nothing to say, that was all. She didn't feel emotional—she would not let herself. There was no point, and no reason to, either.

There was reason only to be glad, to be grateful. Glad beyond any measure she could think of that something so incredibly wonderful had happened to her—and grateful beyond measure to the man who had given her this wonderful, wonderful time, this fantastic gift.

The gift of beauty. The gift of womanhood. The gift of desire. Three precious, precious gifts.

He had given them to her, bestowed them upon her, and they would, she knew, stay with her for ever. She had been allowed into the world that had never let her in before. Oh, it might take a lot of styling, a lot of beautifully designed clothes, a lot of personal grooming that she was not used to, but it could be done—and even without the luxury lifestyle that made it so easy she knew she would never allow herself to relapse into what she had been. A woman in angry exclusion from her womanhood.

Because anyone, anyone at all whom Allesandro di Vincenzo had taken to his bed, could never be excluded from womanhood ever again!

The warm, familiar glow filled her. He'd wanted her—he'd really, really wanted her! It hadn't been fake, or forced, or false. It had been true—absolutely, miraculously true. He had desired her even before he'd known who she was—even before *she'd* known it was her he was seeing in that mirror that first unbelievable evening! And even the shock of discovering just how dramatically, incredibly, the clumpy, frumpy, ugly woman he'd left at the beauty clinic had been transformed, into someone that she could not even recognise herself, had made no difference.

He'd wanted her—plain and simple. Wanted her, desired her, taken her. A man who could have had any woman he liked—and probably had all his life! A man who'd made no secret whatsoever of how much she'd repelled him physically—not rudely, but simply because it had been obviously, glaringly, screamingly obvious, just as it was with all men who saw her that she was a woman who was not one of them, a woman no man would have actually wanted anything to do with.

Her eyes shadowed. Ugliness was a cruel thing—cruel for women, cruel for men too. It was something she'd thought she had to live with, like a deformity—something that would shut her out from the world. But Allesandro had thrown the locked doors open and swept her inside!

And he had changed everything for her. Everything. For ever.

And for that reason she would be grateful to him for ever.

She let her eyes go to him now, as they sped north along the autostrada, his powerful car eating up the miles as effortlessly as his fantastic looks could melt the bones in her body. But it was more than his looks, she acknowledged, incredible as they were—and eyes automatically swept over his sculpted features, the sable hair feathering on his brow—it was much, much more.

After his simmering ill-temper, his clear resistance and reluctance to have anything to do with her, with the situation he'd been forced into by her grandfather, the way he'd been ever since he'd whisked her away had been—well, nothing less than a revelation! It was as if he was a different person. And it wasn't just lust, or sex, or desire, or whatever, that had made him so different with her. It had been... Her brow furrowed with the effort of trying to analyse it, which she hadn't done during their time together. It had been because—well, because he just seemed to enjoy being with her. Spending time with her. Drinking coffee, eating lunch, dinner, breakfast—wandering around the tourist places, strolling along the promenades, along the harbours...

They'd talked—easy stuff, impersonal mostly—and there had been no effort, no strain, no undercurrents—nothing. Just comfortable conversation and comfortable silences. He'd been easygoing, relaxed, good-humoured.

And he'd been like that in bed, too—that was the amazing thing! Oh, he'd been passionate, all right, and had melted her bones all the time, every time, but there had been such a sense of, well, *fun*—it was the only word for it. He'd been so fantastic with her—to her—patient and considerate, as well as mindblowingly sensual, but there'd been laughter as well as passion, good-humoured teasing as well as single-minded intensity.

And always, always, there had been desire. Sometimes nothing more than a wash of appreciation in his eyes, and sometimes a burning focus that had dissolved her to a puddle of weakness in a single searing glance....

Allesandro di Vincenzo, desiring her...

All her life she would know that, know the truth of it.

For all the years ahead...

A coldness snaked through her. Sudden, chilling. Bleak.

No—

Denial. Instant. Strong.

But frightening for all that. Like a sudden vision of winter in midsummer.

Except—the sombre knowledge seeped into her mind—it wasn't midsummer any more. It was autumn already. And it was getting closer to winter with every passing kilometre as they neared Rome. Closer to the point that she just hadn't thought about, because she'd been so totally, completely immersed in simply being with Allesandro—the point at which she would get out of his car and it would be over. Quite, quite over.

For a long, breathless moment she stared ahead, out through the windscreen, her eyes seeing nothing. There was a coldness inside her as if a lump of ice were forming. Abruptly she shut her eyes, shut them tight. No, she must not let herself react like this. She must not. She'd been given a gift—a miraculous gift—and gifts like those should not be accompanied by anything that smacked of ingratitude. Of the recipient saying 'It's not enough! I want more!' like a spoilt child.

And yet...

Her eyes flew open, her head turning to look at Allesandro—as if she were a compass and he magnetic north. The cold sensation came again, and with it something worse, more painful.

I don't want it to be over. It's not enough! I want more!

The cry came from within her, and it shocked her. Scared her. Shamed her. How could she be so greedy, so ungrateful? Wanting another miracle...the miracle of Allesandro not wanting it to be over either...

'Laura—'

His voice in the silence of her painful thoughts made her

start. There was a slight hesitation in it, as though he were about to say something tentative.

'Yes?' She made her voice easy, uncomplicated.

His eyes glanced at her briefly, the returned to the road.

'When we get to Rome…' Again, he hesitated slightly. 'It might be sensible for you simply to stay at my apartment. It's more convenient for my office than the hotel you were staying at.'

She stared at him. Again, he glanced briefly at her, and seeing her blank face he furrowed his brow slightly.

'What is it? Would you rather go back to the hotel?'

She swallowed. His eyes had gone back to the road again. Absently she noticed how the strong, long fingers curled around the edge of the steering wheel.

'Um—' she said.

A smile quirked at his mouth. 'That's it? Um?'

Long-lashed eyes swept over her again, even more briefly.

'It's a very nice apartment,' he supplied helpfully. 'It's a service apartment, so you wouldn't have to cook and clean, you know.' Again the humour quirked. Then, when he went on, his voice changed, becoming more serious. 'The situation's complicated, I know, because of that house of yours in England. But if you can hold on in Rome for, say, another week or so, then I can free myself up workwise to come back with you. If you really do want to keep it, then the best thing would be to appoint an architect and project manager, and let them cope. I'm happy to set that up for you, if you're not sure what's involved. But, having been away from work, I really do need to get some things sorted out—which is why I thought you could simply stay in my apartment till we can both go to England and—'

He broke off, glancing sideways for a second. Laura was staring at him. Her mouth had fallen open.

Lightly he reached out and closed it with one finger, not taking his eyes from the road as he did so.

'What's that American saying? If it ain't broke, don't fix it,' he said cryptically, then changed gear and eased the car effortlessly faster to overtake a lorry. When he finished the manoeuvre he slid back into lane, reached for her hand, raised it to his mouth to brush it lightly, dropped it back again in her lap and said, 'Good—so it's all sorted.'

Then he reached to put some music on.

It filled the car. Filled Laura.

Or something did.

And suddenly it was midsummer again.

CHAPTER FOURTEEN

ALLESANDRO'S apartment was indeed 'very nice', as he had promised. It was the *piano nobile* of an old house in the *centro historico* of Rome, and it was, Laura stared around—a spectacular mix of old architecture and modern interior design.

'Wow,' she breathed.

'I'm glad you like it,' said Allesandro, depositing her luggage. He glanced at his watch. 'Damn. I'm really sorry, but I'm going to have to leave you. I promised my PA I would be in for a meeting by three. Make yourself at home, and I'll phone as soon as I know when I'm going to be clear. A million people will try and grab me because I've been away, but I'll do my best not to be delayed. If you want to go out don't worry about keys. The porter has them, and he speaks good enough English to let you in and out. We'll sort things properly tomorrow.'

He dropped a hasty kiss on her nose, and was gone. Laura stood for a moment, then went to the sash window that over-looked the cobbled internal courtyard of the old building and looked down. Bright splashes of scarlet, pelargoniums in stone urns, brightened the yellowing stone.

There was a strange feeling inside her. The strangest feeling in the world. As if something immense was beginning to form, to seep through her cell by cell, drop by drop. Everything seemed different—as if she were standing on the brink of a new place where she had never been.

Then, like a sunburst through the clouds, that something immense inside her burst into flower—as vivid as the flowers in the courtyard.

Her breath caught and happiness flooded through her like a radiance. Impulsively, instinctively, she whirled round, twirling as if she were wearing a crinoline. Then, abruptly, she stopped. Her eyes widened in alarm.

This wasn't a hotel, and that meant—dismay shot through her—there was no hairdresser here, no beauty salon…. In a handful of hours Allesandro could be back. She had to look her best for him—now more than ever it was imperative!

But she couldn't just wander the streets of Rome, not having a clue where to find a good hairdresser or stylist…

Like a light going on in her brain, she suddenly knew exactly who *would* have a clue. Rifling through her handbag, she found the scrap of paper that Stephanie had scrawled her mobile number on. After a moment or two's hesitation about tackling the Italian phone system all on her own, she made the call.

'*Pronto*—'

'Stephanie?'

'*Si—?*'

'Stephanie, it's Laura. I'm sorry to phone like this, but—'

There was a squeal on the other end of the line. '*Laura?* Where are you?'

'I'm back in Rome, and—'

The squeal came again. 'Oh, that's just *brilliant*! I'm *so* pleased you're back. Listen, stay right where you are and I'll come over and we can catch up on everything. I'll be at your hotel as soon as I can!'

'Er—' This was awkward. With a horrible sense of having fallen headfirst into deep water when she hadn't realised she was by the edge, Laura said haltingly, 'I'm not at the hotel, Stephanie. I'm…er…staying somewhere else at the moment. In the *centro historico*, on the Via Mentone, I think it is. But I can meet you anywhere you—'

There was yet another squeal, but a stifled one. 'The Via

Mentone? But that's where—' Stephanie's voice broke off. Then, in a different tone she said, 'OK, I'm not saying a word—not a *word*! Listen, there's a really nice café just around the corner.' She hurried on to give directions.

As she finished the call, Laura put the phone down slowly. Her thoughts were disturbed. It was one thing to run off to Amalfi with Allesandro—quite another, it seemed, to come back to Rome with him. Stay in his apartment. Be his lover.

Be known and seen as his lover.

Even as the sobering thought came to her, another one penetrated—one she did not want to let in at all. Her grandfather. How would he react—cope—with what had happened between her and Allesandro? With a troubled sigh, she pushed the thought away. She would have to discuss it with Allesandro, she knew. He knew Tomaso far better than she did, and would know how best to handle it. A smile softened her expression. Whatever he thought about her having an affair with Allesandro, her grandfather would, she knew, be happy at her transformation. He had never said a word to her about he way she looked, but she knew that for an old-fashioned old man it would be a great reassurance to know that at last he had a granddaughter who fitted with the world he lived in...

But *did* she fit in? The disturbing question fingered her mind. And as what? Tomaso Viale's long-lost granddaughter? Allesandro di Vicenzo's latest squeeze? And what about Wharton and her responsibilities there? Immediately her thoughts became troubled again, and a sudden spear of longing darted through her that she and Allesandro could just be back in Amalfi again, away from all the complications of their lives.

And the first complication to deal with, she knew, was Stephanie—and just what on earth she was going to say if the girl started grilling her about Allesandro...

But when Laura met her at the designated pavement café, Stephanie said nothing about Allesandro. After responding to Laura's request to make an appointment for her at a salon she could recommend, she chattered on in her friendly, lively, albeit slightly vacuous way, about everything and nothing, mostly about clothes and fashion.

Laura found herself listening with only half an ear. What she was supremely aware of, however, was something she'd not experienced before.

Being eyed up by men.

They were two girls alone, both young and attractive, and it was obvious that every passing Italian male, whatever his age, considered it his social duty to subject them to a thorough appraisal. Laura did her best to emulate Stephanie, who basically ignored the whole thing, but she completely lacked the other girl's practised indifference to the non-stop perusal.

It was as they were just finishing their coffee that Stephanie's indifference suddenly vanished. A youngish man approached them at an angle, across the pedestrianised section of the piazza the café was on, and as he did Stephanie glanced at him, stopped speaking, then parted her lips in a dazzling smile at the man.

'Laura, darling—smile!' she exclaimed.

Bemused, Laura looked where Stephanie was looking, only to see that the man had lifted a camera to his eye. The flash dazzled her momentarily, and she blinked. When she focussed again, the man was gone.

'What—?'

Stephanie gave a laugh. It sounded the slightest bit forced. 'Oh, don't take any notice, darling,' she said airily, 'Roman men are all crazy! Now, we'd better get going. I know you're going to want to look *favolosa* for tonight! Are you going anywhere special?'

'Um—I don't think so,' said Laura. She hadn't the faintest idea what to say, but Stephanie was busy putting down some euros for the coffees, and getting to her feet.

'Let's go!' she said, and started making her way past the tables.

Several hours later, Laura was back in the apartment, musing over a cup of Earl Grey tea she'd found in the kitchen. Allesandro disliked tea, she knew, so was this a previous incumbent's favourite? She put the thought aside. It was the safest thing to do for now. Throughout the extraordinary past week or so she'd done no thinking at all. She'd simply—experienced. It had been all she wanted to do, all she was capable of doing. As if, in a few short days, she was cramming into her life all the years of missing out on what other women took for granted.

As if, too, the sobering thought penetrated again, she were deliberately refusing to think—because to think would be to ask questions, and to ask questions would be to want answers, and answers might be awkward, difficult.

She and Allesandro—so completely different, so much so that anyone would laugh out loud at the thought of the two of them together—had worked amazingly, miraculously, because they had, she knew, quite deliberately created a cocoon about themselves. She knew that he found it unbelievable that he'd taken her to bed, that he'd swept her off to Amalfi, that he'd simply cut loose from everything in his life to spend those amazing, luminous days and nights with her. And she'd found it just as unbelievable too.

But it had worked—crazily, amazingly, fantastically.

Will it work here—back in the real world?

And why did Allesandro want it to? His cryptic words to her in the car echoed strangely in her head—*'If it ain't broke, don't fix it.'*

But what was 'it' anyway? Was it an affair, a relationship? A fling? How could she apply normal words to something that had been so extraordinarily unexpected? How could she think about or analyse or rationalise what had happened?

Then, with a decisive shake of her head, she abandoned her thoughts. She would continue as she had done in Amalfi—taking each wonderful, precious day as it came and nothing more. At least she was ready for Allesandro, whenever he got back here. The salon that Stephanie had taken her to had done wonders, and now she lounged on the pristine white leather sofa in a loose jade-green silk pyjama outfit that felt and looked stunning.

Hopefully, Allesandro would think so too…

A warm, familiar glow filled her, just thinking about him.

I'm here. I'm really here. It isn't over—it's real and continuing and it isn't broken. It's wonderful and fantastic and I am just so, so happy...

Allesandro wanted her. He desired her. Found her beautiful. He had made a woman of her, and because of that she would be a woman for ever now. No more fears, no more mortification or humiliation or sheer, wretched misery as she'd known all her adult life. A misery over which she'd had to plaster like insulating tape layer after layer of antagonism and bitter self-knowledge.

The burden she'd carried all her life was gone. Allesandro had lifted it from her. She hadn't realised it was possible, but he had done it all the same.

And with every touch, every kiss, every caress, every glint in his eye, she'd known, as concretely and definitely as if it had been written in tablets of stone, that he desired her—and if he desired her then, *ergo*, by ineluctable and irrefutable logic, she *was* desirable. He had made her so, and she was.

For ever.

On the table beside her, the phone began to ring. Allesandro— it must be! Carefully setting down her teacup, she picked it up. *Please don't let him say he's working late!*

'Hi!' she said in a warm voice. 'How's it going?'

'Signorina Viale?'

The voice was not Allesandro's. It was a complete stranger's.

'I beg your pardon?' She spoke automatically in English.

'Am I speaking to Laura Stowe-Viale—Tomaso Viale's granddaughter?' The caller spoke English too, but with an Italian accent.

Laura frowned. 'Yes,' she replied. 'Who is this?'

The line went dead. She stared at the receiver a moment, puzzled. Then a noise from the front hall diverted her completely.

Allesandro!

He strode in, tossing his briefcase aside, and scooped her up.

'Miss me?' he grinned. Her answering kiss was all he needed to know, and he carried her through to the bedroom and tumbled her down on the bed with him.

'*Dio*, the perfect end to the day! Everything I want.' His voice was rich with satisfaction. He gazed down at her, his eyes warm and lambent.

She gazed back up at him, happiness streaming from her. He started to kiss her and she was lost. Quite, quite lost. In his arms, she knew with certainty that whatever unease and questioning she might have felt had gone completely. What it was that was happening she could not explain, and did not want to. She knew only, with a deep, abiding assurance, that while she was here, with Allesandro desiring her, she was happy. That was enough.

And nothing could take that away.

Laura gazed out at the infamous Roman traffic through the tinted glass of the car that was taking her to the restaurant where she was meeting Allesandro for lunch. He had woken her with a kiss early that morning, and with an apology.

'I must go already—I have a full board meeting this morning, and today of all days I can't miss it. But I'll be clear for lunch—I'll send a car to collect you at noon.'

She sat back in the seat with happy anticipation, taking out her vanity mirror to check her appearance again. She was getting better at doing her own hair and make up now—more confident. As she stared at herself critically she found herself wondering whether she could see traces of her mother in her. Her mother's beauty, from the photographs her grandparents had kept of her, had been very feminine, softly pretty, with wide, trusting eyes.

No wonder she'd been a push-over for a practised Lothario.

A familiar spurt of loathing filled Laura as she thought of the man who'd fathered her, then never again contacted the woman whose life he'd ruined.

No! I don't want to think about him—I don't want to think about what he did to my mother. He's dead, and it's all far, far too late. All I have to do is be glad, so very, very glad, that I'm not naïve and trusting like my mother was.

Her expression softened. Allesandro was nothing like her father! For what they had together, while it lasted, she could trust him. What they had together was simple, straightforward and honest. Mutual attraction, mutual desire. Nothing else.

She put her vanity mirror away and sat lost in a happy reverie.

'I regret that Signor Viale is not yet here, *signorina*. Would you like a drink while you are waiting?'

She shook her head and took a place on one of several sofas in the restaurant's lobby, where the receptionist was indicating. Feeling self-conscious, for something to do she started to peruse the menu, hoping Allesandro would not be too long...

'Signorina Viale—?'

She looked up. There was a man in a sharp suit who looked vaguely familiar.

'It is Signorina Viale, isn't it?' the man continued. He perched himself on the end of her sofa, placing a folded tabloid-style newspaper in front of her. Her eyes widened.

'It's a good photo, isn't it?' the man said cheerfully.

It was of her and Stephanie, sitting at the café yesterday. There was a headline she couldn't understand, and an article beside it in bold type that was equally incomprehensible. There was another photograph, of Allesandro, and a strange one of a woman in silhouette with a question mark over her. There was also a photograph of Tomaso, and one of a powerboat with a blurred figure at its helm.

'What—?' she began, totally astonished and bewildered.

'Steph couldn't resist tipping me off—she adores being in the papers herself. But even she didn't realise just who you were— only that you'd moved in with Allesandro di Vincenzo. Which of course is a story in itself. But I had my suspicions it was an even bigger story—that's why I phoned the apartment yesterday, to get confirmation, and it got me this scoop! And of course the story's official now.'

His smile was wide. Laura stared at him. 'I don't know what you're talking about. What story?'

He made an airy gesture with his hand. 'It's OK—no one has to speculate any more, so you don't have to do the denial and the stonewalling bit. The press release hit the business section desks this morning, so it's all out in the open. Your fiancé's finally got what he's been after for months now—well, ever since your father was killed. The old man—sorry, your grandfather—resigned yesterday, and this morning's board meeting appointed your fiancé the new chairman.'

She heard only one word.

'Fiancé?'

There was blankness in her voice. But underneath the blankness something else. Something that felt very cold.

'It's perfect, isn't it?' the man was saying, still with that bright smile on his face, and with eyes that, Laura registered with an increase in that cold feeling, weren't actually smiling at all, but were studying her speculatively, assessingly. 'A dream story! Long-lost granddaughter, love at first sight, and a dynastic union to die for! Viale-Vincenzo—partners in love as well as in business. You walk the handsome Allesandro down the aisle and every woman in Rome will envy you, and he gets—at last!— what he's been after. Sole control of Viale-Vincenzo now that he's finally the chairman. Maybe he even gets your father's block of voting shares as a dowry? Who knows? So, next question—when's the wedding? Is it going to be in Rome, or at your grandfather's? Have you chosen a designer for the wedding dress yet? And where's the honeymoon going to be?'

He smiled brightly at her, and there was a sleazy look in his expression, 'Though of course you've already anticipated the honeymoon, haven't you? Romantic days and nights on the Amalfi coast, so I hear. Making sure of you, was he, our handsome Allesandro? What woman could resist him?'

For one long moment Laura just sat there. It seemed endless, but she knew it was only a fraction of a second. A fraction of a second was all that was needed for understanding to hit her.

Understanding of just what Allesandro had done.

It was like a knife going into her with a jagged, serrated edge. And as it came out again it took her guts with her. Hollowing her out.

Sickness flooded into the gaping chasm inside her, and a pain so great she almost gave a gasp from its impact. For a moment she went completely blank, unable to do anything—anything at all.

Then, with a part of her brain that was still working, she realised that someone was walking into the restaurant off the street. Someone she knew.

It was not Allesandro.

Something took her over. An urge for survival—for more than survival. She surged to her feet. 'Luc—darling!' she exclaimed, intercepting him in the doorway, clutching at his arm. 'I don't want to eat here! Can we go somewhere else?'

Her voice was high-pitched, urgent, but she didn't care. Didn't care that for a moment a look of blank astonishment wiped Luc's expression. Then, like a knight in shining armour, he rescued her. He smiled down at her caressingly—intimately.

'Whatever you want, *cara*,' he said, and took her back out onto the pavement.

A taxi was there, and he opened the rear door for her as she all but stumbled inside. Luc came in after her, and her eyes darted to the restaurant door. The tabloid journalist was there, his expression avid. He was taking a camera out of his jacket pocket.

That instinct, the urge for survival—more than survival—stabbed through Laura again. Without conscious volition she wrapped her arms around Luc, and as the taxi started to draw away she kissed him, full on the mouth.

The camera flashed.

Then, pulling back from Luc, who had an unreadable expression on his face, she said, 'Please! Take me to the airport!'

Luc was kind to her. That was the worst of it.

He must know—everyone must know. The tabloid story had spelt the whole thing out in bold type and colour photos. Of course everyone must know!

Everyone except her, that was.

Mortification burned through her as the truth, as harsh, as

pitiless as the truth about herself had always been, stared back hideously at her. The truth that had been there all the time. But she hadn't known it. Hadn't seen it. Had been blinded to it by a stupid, pathetic illusion she'd woven about herself.

That Allesandro had woven...

I thought a miracle had happened! I thought it was real...real! I thought he wanted me! That I'd been transformed, made into a woman he wanted...desired. That I had truly become for him— for me—a woman to desire.

And more than desire.

The jagged knife went into her again.

He wanted me to stay with him! Wanted me to be with him in Rome. He wanted to come to England, for us to be together....

Without her guts inside her, there was only a gaping hollow, devouring her.

I thought what we had was real—

But it hadn't been real at all. Not for a single moment. It had simply been a deliberate, calculated manipulation. She'd been nothing more than a means to an end—an end she had even known he'd wanted! Dear God—she almost choked as the re-alisation hit her—she'd known, *known* he'd wanted the chair-manship of the company! The gaping hollow inside her gaped wider yet. Tomaso had told her how ambitious Allesandro was! Told her that he'd set him the task of bringing her to him. And she'd known exactly what he'd been prepared to do to get her there. Ruthlessly bribe her. And then, yet again, when Tomaso had wanted her to go to Rome Allesandro had just as ruthlessly threatened her with demanding his loan back again!

Her eyes widened in pain. She'd had all the evidence of just how ambitious, how ruthless he was in front of her—and yet he'd fooled her. Still fooled her.

Because I wanted to be fooled!

The answer came, cold and cruel. Mortifying and humiliat-ing. Burning like acid on her skin.

I wanted to be fooled! I wanted to be like all the others—one of the beautiful people! Worthy of a man like Allesandro! I wanted it so much! I wanted him to want me, desire me. I wanted to believe he thought the miracle true. I wanted it so badly...

And he'd played on it ruthlessly—just as ruthlessly as he'd played on her need for money for Wharton. He'd known exactly how to manipulate her.

The chill went through every vein as she realised every last hideous, mortifying truth. Just as Tomaso had known how to manipulate Allesandro, how to get him to do one last task for him.

Provide the ideal husband for Tomaso's ugly, unmarriageable granddaughter.

And sweeten the poison pill by rewarding him with control of the company.

She shut her eyes against it, but it was no good. The truth burned through her eyelids. The truth she could not hide from. The truth she could never hide from.

The truth she had to face. The truth that it had all been nothing but a lie. Nothing but a way to get what he really wanted. Not her. Never her.

Never me.

The words tolled in her brain. Pain laced through her.

And then into the pain came something else. Something familiar. As familiar as a worn suit of armour. She felt it slipping over her—the armour she had worn all her life. The armour—a last, searing stab of pain went through her—she would now wear again.

It was never you. It will never be you.

She could feel her expression hardening. Taking on old, familiar lines. No, it would never be her. She knew that. She had always known it. There was nothing new about it. Nothing different.

And nor was she.

Her face set, eyes hard, slowly she turned her head. Luc was watching her, and she could see the sympathy in his eyes. Automatically, her chin lifted. She'd seen sympathy in men's eyes before. The kind men, who felt sorry for a woman who looked the way she did. She hadn't thought Luc was one of them, but it seemed she was wrong. But then—another stab went through her guts—it was so easy for her to be wrong about men...

So easy for them to fool her by playing on what she so desperately wanted to be true.

For a moment a rage burst in her that almost overpowered her. A rage to storm in and confront Allesandro—hurl at him just how *contemptible* he was to do what he had! To make such an abject, pathetic fool of her! *Use* her to advance his career—

Then, as swiftly as it had come, the rage died away. What would be the point? None—none at all. It would change nothing. Certainly not the truth.

As she met Luc's eyes, guilt went through her. She'd used him shamelessly just now—used him with a ruthlessness that was unforgivable. As unforgivable as the ruthlessness Allesandro had used on her…

'I'm sorry!' The words blurted from her. 'I'm sorry that I—that I—'

He shook his head. 'It's OK. I recognised Stephanie's tame hack back there.' There was a questioning look in his eye. 'I take it he got the story wrong?'

Her face hardened again.

'Yes,' she said tersely. She didn't say anything more. There wasn't anything to say. She closed up on herself like a clam.

Feeling bad that she had commandeered Luc like this, she started to say that if he would stop the taxi she would continue to the airport on her own, but he overruled her.

'Allow me,' he said. 'I take it you are returning to England?'

She nodded, hands clenched in her lap. It didn't matter that she had nothing with her but her handbag—it had her passport, wallet and house keys in it, which was all she needed to get home.

Home! Home to Wharton. Where she would be safe. Where she had always been safe. A refuge, a hiding place from the world.

A sanctuary.

Desperately needed. More than she had ever needed it in her life.

The knife thrust came again.

More than she had ever dreamt she would need it in her life.

* * *

Allesandro picked up the paperweight on his desk, then put it down again. Very carefully. It took a lot of control to do so. A lot of control to stop him hurling it right through the plate-glass window of the chairman's office—his office now that Tomaso had finally made good on his promise and retired—and hoping it might just land on Luc Dinardi.

The far too familiar bolt of white fury went through him as he thought of Luc. But the bolt that followed was just as familiar. And far, far worse.

Dio, *how could she have done it? How could she?*

But she had. That was all. She'd walked out of his apartment and into the arms of Luc Dinardi. Then flown off to London. That poisonous article in the trashy tabloid had made it all perfectly clear—as had the photo of Laura kissing Luc in the taxi.

Why—why had she done it?

There was only one answer he could give. Only one that fitted.

I gave her a taste for sex, and she couldn't wait to try it out with the next man walking past...

His jaw clenched grittily as he fought back the fury. He would not let it out. Would keep everything tight—tightly nailed down. Let nothing out.

And he wouldn't think about her, or what she had done.

Impatiently, he yanked a leather bound folder in front of him. He'd get some work done. God knew there was enough of it now that he was chairman of Viale-Vincenzo! His mouth twisted bitterly. What was that saying? If the gods want to punish you, they give you what you want?

Well, once he had thought he wanted the chairmanship— wanted it so badly he'd put up with Tomaso's machinations and manipulations. Though it was ironic—so deeply, bitterly ironic!— that Tomaso's final plan, thinking to bribe him with his resignation at last if he took his granddaughter to Rome, had not been the reason he'd done so! Tomaso might assume it was, but Allesandro knew he had brought Laura to Rome, taken the gamble he had by handing her over to that beauty clinic, in order to get *out* of the infernal trap Tomaso had sprung on him, which would have made him look like the biggest louse in Rome. *That* was why he'd done it! Not because of the chairmanship. Never for that!

Yet he'd got the chairmanship as well.

Emotion showed briefly in his eyes. Stabbing, like a knife wound. Yes, he'd got the chairmanship—and it was dust and ashes in his mouth!

Dust and ashes after what Laura had done to him.

How could she do it? How could she just walk out like that? *I thought… I thought…*

The emotion stabbed in his eyes again.

Yes, he'd thought. Thought. Imagined.

That was all it had been. It hadn't been real—it hadn't been real at all. He'd just imagined that Laura had wanted him as much as—amazingly, incredibly—he'd wanted her! That it had meant as much to her as it had to him. That, like him, she had—

No! Don't go there—stop right now!

He felt, crazily, that he was standing on the edge of a precipice. A precipice he must not plummet over. Or he would smash himself to pieces on jagged, vicious rocks.

And he would not smash himself. Nor would he smash the paperweight. His fingers closed over it. For a second—a second only—they clenched, and then, with complete control, he picked it up, and slid it inside a desk drawer.

Safer out of sight.

Like Laura.

CHAPTER FIFTEEN

THE builders were booked for the following day, but with the rain still coming down in rods there was little chance they would arrive. Frustration bit at Laura. She wanted to get on with things—with getting the work on Wharton started. She needed to get stuck into it. Soaking up her energy, her thoughts. Occupying her. Distracting her.

She'd been back for a fortnight now, and the first thing she'd done was to finalise the mortgage she needed and book the builders. She had set up the lengthy schedule of work that needed doing before winter came round—a lot of it by herself, as well as by professionals. It would be arduous, and complicated and back-breaking, but she didn't care. She welcomed it.

Restoring Wharton was, after all, all she had now.

But it was all you had before I went out to Italy anyway! So stop feeling sorry for yourself. Stop making a fuss. Nothing's changed—you're right back where you started from. You haven't lost anything—you're the same as you always were!

The bitter, galling truth stung through her.

Yes, that was the truth of it—the inescapable, bitter truth. She was the same as she always had been.

And she always would be.

Delia was back from the Caribbean. She was looking sleek and tanned as she swanned up to Allesandro at the party he'd forced himself to go to.

'Guido was a bore,' she informed him, and laid a hand possessively on his sleeve. 'I really missed you, Sandro—' She pouted seductively.

Allesandro removed the hand. 'Delia, *cara*,' he said, not bothering to conceal the edge in his voice, 'forget it. It's over.' He nodded at her curtly, and moved away.

Immediately he was conscious of the eyes of at least three other females in the vicinity going to him with speculative interest. Irritation spiked through him. Why the hell couldn't they leave him alone? Did he have some sign over his head saying, 'Come and get me'? No, he did not. Did he have a sign saying, 'In the market for pointless sex with someone I couldn't care less about'? No. And he definitely didn't have one saying 'Deserted for Luc Dinardi'.

His mouth compressed to a tight line, and he stood, staring broodingly, balefully, telling himself an essential truth..

You made an idiot of yourself—that was all! You were so stunned at her transformation that you acted like an idiot. As for her, you obviously gave her a taste for it! No man had ever looked once at her, let alone twice, and once she realised that she'd been let loose in a candy store, she decided to try out the candy bars. All the candy bars—not just yours. Starting with Luc Dinardi...

She's probably helped herself to half a dozen more candy bars since then.

She's probably—

'Allesandro.' The voice behind him made him turn, his thoughts cutting out. As he saw who had addressed him, a frown crossed his brow. It was Ernesto Arnoldi. 'I would like to speak to you a moment. Somewhere more private. Would you oblige me?'

Allesandro's automatic response was to refuse, but courtesy made it impossible. With a brief nod, he followed Arnoldi to a deserted room, away from the party. What on earth could Stefano's friend have to say to him?

For a moment the older man said nothing, then he spoke. 'I

have been considering whether to do this, but I think I must.' He paused again, as if weighing his words. 'I realised, you understand, right from the start, who Laura Stowe was. You see, Stefano had told me about her. Tell me...' The pause, the slightest hesitation, came again. 'What does she think about her father?'

Allesandro eyed him straightly. There was a sombreness about the man he had not seen before. Nevertheless, he answered the question. His voice was not warm as he spoke.

'She thinks as much as anyone would think about a man who seduced their mother and then refused to take responsibility for the outcome.'

Again there was a pause, and again Ernesto Arnoldi made the decision to speak.

'There is something she should know about Stefano,' he said heavily. 'Something that may...help her.'

Allesandro stilled.

Laura was sawing logs in the woodshed, the sound of the rain spattering on the slate tiles inaudible above the noisy roar of the electric saw. It was tiring work, and as she finally cut the motor to start loading the logs into the wheelbarrow the ache in her back intensified.

But it was not the ache in her back that hurt.

The pain was somewhere quite different. A place that had no right to hurt. None at all.

As she wheeled the barrow across the yard, she heard the sound of a car approaching along the front drive. She stopped dead. No one visited via the front drive. The last person to do so had been—,

Her breath stopped. Then, with monumental effort, she parked the full wheelbarrow in the kitchen porch, pulled off her Wellington boots and marched through the house to the front door. She yanked it open. A silver saloon was parked, and someone was getting out. Someone who was as out of place this time around as he had been the first time he had walked into her life.

But now she had walked out of *his* life. Out of his plans and schemes and lies and deceits.

Even in the short distance between the car and the front porch the rain had got to work, making diamonds in the sable hair. Hair she had once brushed with her fingers...

He had stepped onto the porch, and instinctively she took a step backwards, using the door as a barricade. Her heart had started to pound. It made her angry.

'What are you doing here?' she demanded. She didn't bother to hide her anger.

Answering anger flashed in his face. Emotion was running in her—not just anger, more than that. Worse than that. Shock, too, in a great big slug to her head that was making her stupid. And angry.

'I have something to say to you,' Allesandro ground back brusquely.

He didn't want to be here, where it was still raining, where it did nothing but rain. Above all he didn't want to say anything to Laura, or see her again.

Didn't want to see a woman who'd taken his breath away when she'd been transformed into a stunning, show-stopping beauty. A woman who'd turned his head. More than his head...

A woman who had just used him as an experiment, to get the taste for sex, who'd then gone on to try it out on the rest of his sex. Starting with Luc Dinardi. And God knew who else she'd tried it with since him!

But as his eyes took in her appearance, standing there belligerently at the front door, he realised that whatever she was getting up to now, it wasn't that. The new Laura that he'd so disastrously created had disappeared.

She'd reverted. It was the only word for it. Her hair was hanging in lank, soggy rags round her face, she wore no make-up, her eyebrows were overgrown, her skin blotchy, and she was wearing some abomination of a pair of trousers in baggy cord and a shapeless waxed jacket The old Laura was back—the one who was a million miles away from the Laura he'd called into being. The one who'd bowled him over, swept him away—made a total fool of him. Angry relief stabbed through him. He was glad, savagely glad that she'd turned back into the old Laura. The one he didn't want—that no man could possibly want.

The savagery stung through him again. *Dio*, Luc Dinardi wouldn't be sliming around after her now if he could see her! She wouldn't have a bat's chance in hell of waltzing off with him! Getting herself plastered in a face-to-face clinch with him all over a trashy tabloid by some sleazy paparazzi! Luc Dinardi would run a hundred miles now! Any man would. He would too, but he didn't have a damn choice. And the lack of choice made him angry.

Why the hell am I always ending up here when I don't want to—doing someone else's dirty business? First for Tomaso, now for Stefano...

Laura was glaring at him. Her veins were fizzing. Heart pounding. What the hell did Allesandro di Vincenzo have to be angry about? Except the fact that she hadn't proved, after all, to be the idiot he'd thought she was! The gullible fool. The pathetic, impressionable half-wit....

'Well, whatever it is, say it and go!'

His mouth pressed tightly. A mouth she had kissed a hundred times...

'It is not something to say on a doorstep. It concerns your—'

'*Tomaso!*' Laura's cry of alarm cut through his words.

His expression changed slightly, and he shook his head. Diamond drops flew.

'No—Tomaso is fine. Well—' his face darkened again '—as fine as can be expected, given your behaviour.'

Laura's eyes flashed fire. '*My* behaviour! Good God, you've got a bloody nerve!'

Dark brows snapped together. 'You stand there and say that to me? After the way you behaved?'

'The way *I* behaved? I don't *believe* you're standing there accusing *me*!'

A hand slashed through the air. '*Basta!* This I not why I am here. I am here for one reason only.' He took a harsh breath. 'It's about your father.'

Immediately her face closed. It was a familiar expression. He'd seen it on her face often enough.

'Whatever it is, I don't want to know,' she said mutinously, rejectingly.

Allesandro's expression became grimmer. 'Yes,' he said, 'you do. And I have no intention of telling you here on your doorstep. So let me in.'

Grudgingly, she pulled the front door open. He strode in, and cast his eyes around disparagingly.

'I'm waiting for the builders,' she said, with more defensiveness than she felt she owed. 'The weather's been too wet for them to start work.'

She headed across the hall to the baize door that led through to the kitchen. Allesandro followed with a sense of dim familiarity. Warmer, but still shabby. He pulled out a rickety chair and sat down. He watched as Laura dumped herself heavily, ungracefully, in another, shrugging off her jacket. Roughly she pushed her lank, dripping hair back.

Out of nowhere, memory intruded into Allesandro's vision. Laura—new Laura, incredible Laura, stunning Laura—walking towards him in the bar of the hotel that first, unbelievable night, looking as if she could stop traffic.

Why the hell has she let herself go again?

The question sprang in his mind. Why on earth had she let herself revert? She knew what she could look like, so why go back to what she had once been? And she knew her power as a woman now—so why bury herself here in this rain-sodden dump?

Well, what did he care? Nothing, that was what! He'd done with Laura Stowe—old or new. He would say what he had to say, let her make of it what she would, and then he would go. Clear off. Back to Rome. Where there were beautiful women by the score who wanted him, who wouldn't be in his bed one morning and in Luc Dinardi's arms by lunchtime!

'Well, what is this burningly important thing you have to tell me that you've come all this way to say?'

Her curt question cut through his baleful thoughts. He took a breath. 'Do you remember that man we met at the Bellini reception at the hotel in Rome? The one I told you knew your father?'

Her face darkened even more, and he saw her hands tense on the table. 'Yes. I didn't like him. What about him?'

For a moment Allesandro was silent, then he said, 'He asked me to tell you something about your father.'

'I don't want to know!' she retorted tightly.

Allesandro ignored her. 'What I am going to tell you,' he said slowly, 'may help you to understand why he made the decisions he did all those years ago. It may not excuse your father, but it may…' his eyes rested on her '…explain him.'

She was staring at him, inexpressive, her closed, shuttered face giving nothing away. Locking herself away inside her head, behind the face that looked out blankly on the world, repelling all boarders. He'd forgotten how she could look like that— holding the world at bay.

Defying it.

Defying it with the plainness of her face—a face that people would not want to look at, that held no welcome or attraction. People might pity her, or question her about why she had no father, why no man had ever acknowledged that she was his daughter, or why she was living with her mother's parents, who were, despite their love for her, ashamed of her existence. Ashamed that their beloved daughter had got herself pregnant by some Latin lothario, blighting all hopes of a normal life by burdening herself and her family with a bastard, nameless baby…

It's her defence, her protection—her armour.

The understanding came like a strange, distorted light. But he had no time to comprehend it further.

'Go on.' Her voice was still curt, indifferent, but the hands on the table had stiffened, fingers indenting into the surface of the wood.

'This may be a shock to you,' he said slowly, trying to pick his words carefully, but knowing it was impossible, 'for it was certainly one to me, but Stefano, it seems, led a double life—a life no one knew about. He and Ernesto were very clever in their concealment of it.'

He took a deep breath. She was looking at him, but her face was still expressionless, still closed and shuttered.

How can she look so different from when she was with me? There, then, she was so open—her face said everything that she felt! She was completely transparent!

Except—the thought sobered him—that she had not been transparent at all in the end. He had thought he'd known her, but he hadn't—not at all. He had left her as one person—and hours later she had been someone else. Someone he had called into being without knowing it. Someone who had made him angrier than he had believed possible. Because it *was* anger, obviously, that he felt about her. Not because she had dared to make the most of the discovery of who she could be, how she could look, but because she had given no indication—not the least—that she was moving on to another man...

Was I so damn unimportant to her?

The pointless question needed no answer. Of course he'd been that unimportant...

Just as now he was nothing more than a messenger.

A messenger who still had to deliver his message. Deliver it, and get out. It was up to her what she made of it. It wasn't his business. *She* wasn't his business.

Just say what you came to say and go!

His inner thoughts admonished him. For the last time he eye-balled Laura, straight in her closed, inexpressive eyes, and said, 'Your father refused to answer your mother's pleadings, refused to acknowledge your existence, because he felt Tomaso would pressure him into marrying your mother. He couldn't do that because—' he took a deep breath, and said it, 'he was gay. He and Ernesto were lovers. They kept it a secret—making it look as though they were both libertines, running a licentious life-style—but it was fake. The whole thing. They didn't want to admit it. Stefano didn't want his father to know. He was ashamed of what he was. He would rather be thought a libertine and a playboy than a homosexual.'

She wasn't saying anything, wasn't reacting.

Doggedly, Allesandro ploughed on, relaying the message from Ernesto Arnoldi about her father, just as he had relayed the message from her grandfather when he had first set foot in this benighted dump. A messenger boy—that was all he was. And thank God for it. Thank God that all he had to do was relay his message and then get out. *Out.* So he didn't have to face Laura again. Whatever she looked like. Whichever version of herself she was—new or old.

He never wanted to face her again.

'Ernesto told me that it was only once that Stefano was desperate to try and disprove the truth about himself. It was with your mother. She was young, inexperienced with men, a visitor who would soon be gone again. He would force himself to have sex with her, and prove he wasn't gay. But all it did…' his voice changed '…was prove the opposite. Convince him that he was.' He took another breath. 'That was why he refused to get back in touch with her when she wrote to him that she was pregnant. He knew Tomaso would make him marry her. He could not face that.'

He was silent a moment, then went on, finishing his message. 'If it is the slightest consolation to you, Ernesto told me that your father checked that your mother had been taken in by her family, that you were being raised by your grandparents. That you did not need him.'

Her face was still expressionless. Then her eyes flickered to the window, looking out sightlessly. For a long moment she did not speak.

When she did, her voice was strained.

'I never thought I could feel sorry for my father. I've hated and despised him for so long—all my life.' Her gaze suddenly went back to Allesandro. 'But to feel ashamed of what you are is—'

She fell silent, and looked away again. Then she blinked

rapidly and stood up, pushing back her chair. Her chin went up, and she looked directly at Allesandro. Slowly he got to his feet as well.

'Thank you for telling me.' Her voice was jerky. 'Tell *Signor* Arnoldi that...that I thank him too. Perhaps I should do so myself. I'm sure you don't appreciate being dragged into this. Do you have a contact address for him? Or perhaps I should phone. He won't want anything in writing—not if he's tried so hard all these years to conceal—'

She broke off. Swallowed. Then recovered, her chin jutting tensely.

'I'm sorry you had to come here. I know you wouldn't have wanted to.'

Her voice was tight. Against his will, Allesandro heard himself speak.

'Are you all right?'

Her eyes snapped suddenly. 'Of course I'm all right! Like you said—it doesn't excuse my father's behaviour, but at least it explains it. And I can understand what it's like to be ashamed of what you are, to know that others are...would be...ashamed of you too, even if they love you. So I'm glad I know about my father. Know that he could never have married my mother, and that if he had it would have been a disaster anyway. So I don't have to hate him any more. I can just get on with my life. I've got a lot to keep me busy right now anyway. Getting this house restored. Starting the holiday lettings business. All that stuff.'

'Too busy to bother with your grandfather? You've just cut him out of your life again!'

There was accusation in Allesandro's voice.

Her expression flared. 'Let's just say I'm not feeling too charitably disposed to him right now, shall we? What he tried to do was as despicable as what you did!'

'*Como?*' Allesandro's eyes flashed in disbelief. 'What are you *talking* about?'

'Oh, don't bother to deny it!' she retorted scathingly. The lid had come off her emotions. Suddenly, out of nowhere, rage was boiling up in her. Boiling over. Rage that had been banked down and hammered down and held down with a lid so tight she had never wanted to let it explode.

But now it had. Emotion flooded from her—anger, fury, rage—it had to be that. It *had* to be!

'That paparazzo that Stephanie tipped off told me all about it! All about the cosy little arrangement you and Tomaso cooked up so you could finally get him to give up being chairman and you could run the whole company yourself.'

Dark brows snapped together. 'What paparazzo? When? As for Tomaso's scheming—I told you about it myself when we reached the health spa! You agreed—finally!—to go along with it. And don't tell me you weren't happy to do so when you realised you could! You jumped in with both feet! Like a kid in a candy store! You took to it like a natural!'

She backed away, face belligerent, contorted.

'And you made sure of it, didn't you? Making such a pathetic fool of me! You must have known I'd be a complete push-over! It was despicable of you! Totally despicable! If that paparazzo hadn't blown the whistle on you—'

'*What* paparazzo? The one who took the photo of you kissing Luc Dinardi?'

'As it happens, yes! He was the one that accosted me in that restaurant and opened my eyes to what was really going on, to what I'd been too bloody stupid to see! He asked me when our wedding was!'

Allesandro stilled. 'He did *what*?'

'He asked me,' Laura ground out, 'when our wedding was. Now that you had the damn chairmanship finally in the bag!'

Allesandro stood quite motionless. 'He said that, did he?'

'Yes!' Laura threw her head up, crossing her arms across her chest, her shoulders squaring back angrily. 'He did. He said a press release had gone out that morning, saying you were now chairman and Tomaso had resigned. So *obviously* you were going to marry me to keep your side of the bargain you struck with my damn grandfather! Something everyone seemed to know about and to be expecting—except, of course, stupid, stupid me.'

Allesandro's eyes had narrowed. Every muscle in his body was tense. Tenser than they'd ever been in his life.

'Let's get this straight, absolutely straight, shall we? You believe that Tomaso said he would only resign if I married you? Is that right?'

'Yes,' she hissed. 'And when the light finally, *finally* went off in my head suddenly everything was crystal clear! My God, it took me long enough to see it, but when I did, then it all made sense!'

'Did it? I'm pleased to hear it.' Allesandro's voice was measured. His very calmness seemed to infuriate her more.

'Oh, *good*!' she snarled back at him. 'Then you'll be just as pleased, won't you, to hear what I think of a man who stoops so low he's prepared to force himself to have sex with a woman he doesn't want just to get control of a company? And haven't you damn well been *lucky*? Thanks to that paparazzo who told me what the hell was going on, you didn't even have to end up actually having to *marry* me! For the sake of a short, brief farce, and having to take me to bed for a week, you ended up with the chairmanship in the bag—*and* you're still footloose and fancy-free at the end of it all!'

She took a juddering breath and seared on. 'And if you had to put up with having that photo of me and Luc plastered all over the tabloids—and, boy, do I hope it was!—then *tough*! Now *you* know what it's like to be made a fool of! The way you made a complete fool of me!'

She gave a hard, heavy sigh. Suddenly her fury was spent. Gone. Emptied out.

The way she was emptied out.

Misery filled its place. Bleak and bitter.

And pointless—so, so pointless. Just as this whole vicious exchange was pointless. The truth was what it was. Just as she was what she was.

Nothing could change it.

She shook her head with impatient weariness. 'Oh, for God's

sake—what does it matter anyway? It's over and done with. There's no point going over it. You wanted that damn chairmanship, you did everything Tomaso told you to do, and you've ended up with exactly what you wanted. So bully for you. Apart from soft soaping me into bed and gritting your teeth during sex and thinking of the chairmanship, the only price you had to pay was a stupid photo in a stupid tabloid that no one with any brains would read anyway, probably, so who cares? I'm out of your hair, and you've done your last duty—delivered your last message. Now you can just go, can't you? At last. So—go. Go on, go! I've got work to do. Mountains of stuff. So just go.'

Her voice fell at the end, and she stared blankly at him. He still hadn't moved. It irritated her. Irritated the hell out of her. She wanted him gone. He could take his elegant, designer-suited male perfection out of her house, climb back into his expensive hire car and drive away, back to Rome—go and chair some meetings, since he was so keen on being chairman. So damn keen he'd gone and had her dressed up like some stupid, embarrassing doll, and then forced himself to take her to bed, knowing she'd be a total push-over—because how on earth could any woman say no to a man who looked like him, who kissed like him, who—?

'Just *go!*' Her voice was a stifled yell. 'Go on! I don't want you here! I don't want you anywhere near me! I don't want anything more to do with you! Or my grandfather! Or Italy! So just *go!*'

The trouble was, he wasn't going. He was just standing there. Then he was doing something even worse. He was closing the distance between them.

'I did *not*,' Allesandro said, biting out each word, 'have sex with you, as you so charmingly put it, for any reason to do with becoming chairman of Viale-Vincenzo. That you should for a single moment allow yourself to believe what some gutter paparazzo says to you I find—' he took a sharp intake of breath '—unbelievable. That you should then storm straight off to another man I find—unforgivable.'

His pupils had narrowed to points.

'How could you do it? How could you go from me to him in

the space of a single day? Just because you believed, like a half-wit, what some half-baked hack had told you? How could you even credit such preposterous idiocy and think what you did? That Tomaso was trying to get me to marry you and bribing me with the chairmanship.'

'You're telling me he *didn't*?' she hurled back at him scornfully.

'All Tomaso did was try and get me to take you to Rome by dangling his damn letter of resignation. But that was *not* why I took you! I insisted on your going for a completely different reason!'

'Like *what*?' she demanded disbelievingly.

For a moment he did not answer, then, 'Tomaso had deliberately spread that rumour—the one suggesting I was on the point of marrying his granddaughter, whom no one in Rome had yet laid eyes on. So I took you to Rome for my own purpose.'

Her eyes flashed hatred.

'Yes, I know. I know *exactly* why you took me to Rome! And why you swept me off to Amalfi! *And* why you installed me in your apartment! Why you made a complete and absolute fool of me! So don't you *dare* stand there and throw Luc Dinardi in my face! Because he was a whole lot *kinder* to me than you were! He let me kiss him to give that disgusting reporter that photo, and he did it because he felt sorry for me. Sorry because you'd made such a fool of me. Making me think…making me think—'

Her voice choked into silence, her throat like a vice. She wanted to shut her eyes. Shut him out of her sight. But she couldn't. She could only go on staring at him. Seeing everything about him—the sculpted planes of his face, the winged line of his eyebrows, the long sweep of his lashes, the high cut of his cheekbone, the smooth indentation between his nose and the edges of his mouth.

His mouth…

She wanted to look away. Needed to look away. But she couldn't.

I kissed him, embraced him, made love to him, held him in my arms, held him against my heart…

Pain knifed through her—that jagged, serrated pain again, tearing out her guts.

But it wasn't me who did those things, who did so much else—who laughed, and talked, and stood quietly watching the sun set over the sea, my arms around him, watching the moon sail overhead. It wasn't me—

It was someone who didn't exist. Who can't exist. I thought she could, but she doesn't. She can't. She's just in my imagination, that's all.

My fantasy. My fantasy of being beautiful—of having the most wonderful man in the world look on me with desire, with wanting, with something even more precious...

From somewhere deep inside, she found a strength she hadn't known she had. Her chin lifted. Unflinchingly, resolutely, she spoke.

'But I'm not a fool any longer. I can't be. I know the truth, and it's what it's always been. All my life.'

She faced him, cheeks mottled with staining colour, hair lank, eyes hard. The woman she'd always been, all her life. Her voice was flat as she went on, spelling out the truth.

'I wanted to believe you'd turned me into a swan, but you hadn't. You couldn't. It wasn't possible. This is the real me—now, here—and that's that. Nothing's going to change. It doesn't matter what they do to me, the hairstyles or the clothes. This is the real me, like this. Nothing to be done about it. Just like my wretched father couldn't do anything about what he was. He just had to accept it. "What can't be cured must be endured," my grandmother used to say. And it's true. They had a lot to endure, my mother's parents, and they did it without complaining. Their daughter "got into trouble", as they saw it, and then died, and they had to bring me up—and everyone knowing I was their bastard, fatherless granddaughter. At least they knew I wouldn't—couldn't—follow in my mother's footsteps. That I'd never bring a double helping of shame on them. They were grateful I looked the way I do. That I could never be a swan. That I accepted the truth about myself.'

Allesandro was looking at her—looking at her strangely.

'They were grateful, Laura, for something quite different.' His voice seemed harsh suddenly. 'They were grateful—' his eyes never left her, held her implacably '—because you accepted the *lie* about yourself. Their lie. The lie they built up for you, year after year.' His expression changed minutely, became momentarily less harsh. 'Oh, they did it for reasons they thought were good ones. They did it to keep you safe, as you yourself say, from the fate that overcame your mother. But it was a lie. All the time—a lie.'

He took a step towards her and she tensed unbearably. His voice as he spoke was infused with urgency. His eyes held hers still.

'Listen—listen to me, Laura. You think I cynically, calculatingly did Tomaso's bidding. But if what you've accused me of is *not* true, as I say it is not, then neither is the truth you see about yourself. The truth that only you see. The same truth that I saw right until that moment when a completely new truth about you totally destroyed it. For ever. For *ever*, Laura. That moment when I realised that the woman I saw in the entrance to the bar was *you* changed you for ever. Changed you into the person you should have been all along. Could have been if your grandparents hadn't been so frightened for you. Terrified you would repeat your mother's fate. They did it for love of you, I'm sure, but they made you think there was no escape from the girl you always saw. The one they made sure you were. The one you went on making yourself out to be.'

He took a breath. A long one. His eyes still held hers. Would not let them go. She stared, eyes still pained, noose still tight.

'You were so very convincing,' he said. There was a new note in his voice. It was bizarre to think it so, but it was, she could not deny it, almost wry. 'You certainly convinced me. Oh, you had help, no doubt about that. Those abominable clothes, those heavy shoes you clumped around in. The hairstyle from hell. The complete and absolute lack of any attempt at grooming. And the resentment, Laura—coming off you in great, ugly waves. Resentment and defiance. Cussedness. Stubbornness. Obstinacy. Damning the world.' He paused. 'Because you'd damned yourself.'

His eyes would not let her go. Would not let her do anything but stand there, while the noose was like a death-clutch around her throat.

'And it was a lie. A lie the whole time. A lie of your own persistence. You weren't that person at all. You were someone completely different. Someone I saw that night. And it blew me away—just blew me away.' His expression changed. Softened. Became, with the timbre of his voice, the glint in his eye, reminiscent. 'Someone I saw every day and every night. A completely different person. Freed from the lie.'

He took a step towards her. She did not move. Could not move.

'You'll have to choose your lie now, Laura. You realise that, don't you? Either the idiocy of me seducing you to get that infernal chairmanship, which I never, *never* did, is a lie, or else that the Laura standing here right now is a lie. The Laura who looks like something that got left out in the rain or got found in the trash can. You can't have both lies, Laura. And I know why you chose the lie you did. Because if you thought I was just after the chairmanship, then it meant I never really wanted you—and that meant you were really still the old Laura, the Laura you're trying to be again, because it's the Laura you've known all your life.'

He took another step towards her, and still she did not move. Could not move.

Still the dark, long-lashed eyes held hers, would not let her go. No matter how tight the noose around her neck.

'But I didn't take you to bed to get the chairmanship. I took you to bed because I wanted to. Because you are a beautiful, desirable woman. And you are more, Laura. So much more.'

His eyes had changed now, but she still could not move, and there was still a noose around her throat. But it was different now. A silken noose.

'We were good together, Laura. The best. It just worked. Clicked. Whatever. I didn't want it to end. I didn't want it to stop. I didn't want to think about Tomaso, or how I was going to tell him what was happening between us. Or about the company. Or anything. I just wanted to go on with what we had. Different from anything I've known. And since you left I've been raging.

Furious. Angry. Livid. With you, because I thought you so shallow that you could walk from my bed to another man. With Luc for being that other man. But mostly with myself. For taking your desertion so badly. It shouldn't have got to me the way it did.'

'I can't imagine many women walk out on you, Allesandro,' she managed to get out.

The wry look came in his face again.

'The woman before you walked out on me—and all I felt was irritation. When you walked out on me I felt—devastation. And it's only now I can see why. Can you see why?'

'No,' she said. Because it was the only thing she could say. Dared say.

'Then I will show you,' he said.

He stepped towards her. There was a split second of denial in her, and then, like a shockwave, she realised what he was going to do.

He slid his fingers underneath the lank lumps of hair either side of her face and cradled her head. Her breath caught. She felt too weak and helpless to jerk away, which she knew she must do, *must* do....

But she couldn't. She just couldn't...

He was gazing down at her. Gazing down with those dark, beautiful, long-lashed eyes that she could drown in—had drowned in, over and over again, when he'd wrought that miracle on her, taken her through the doors that had forever been barred to her. Gazing down at her as though the miracle were still true, and not the cruel, cruel deception that she now knew it to be, had known ever since that paparazzo had, with one intrusive, destructive question, ripped the stupid illusion from her and shown her what a stupid, gullible, pathetic fool she had been taken for...

'Close your eyes.' The low, accented voice tightened the noose around her throat. 'Close your eyes—and I shall close mine.'

She let her eyes fall shut. Not to obey, only to shut out, somehow, anyhow—the awfulness of gazing into those eyes that could drown her in an instant. As her eyes fluttered shut the world went dark around her, and she felt the tips of his fingers move.

Every cell in her body stilled. Motionless.

His fingers moved. Exploringly, searchingly. Over the contours of her face, across the swell of her lips, down over the column of her neck.

And suddenly, out of nowhere, dissolving through the reality of her kitchen, the rain on the windows, the bleak, gritted anger inside her, she was back—back in Italy, in Sorrento, in Rome, back in that magical, miraculous world that had opened its gates to her...

Welcoming her in. Accepting her.

Wanting her.

The noose around her throat was gone. The anger was gone, and all that it had hidden was gone.

She felt his mouth brush hers. Like the wings of a butterfly.

'Laura,' he said, breathed.

And then he kissed her.

Softly and sensuously. She thought she must surely die of it.

And she was his again, *his*, and he was embracing her, caressing her, wanting her and desiring her—because she was a woman for him to desire, for the most beautiful man in the world to desire...

He drew his mouth away, but his fingers still cradled her face, upturned to his. Her eyes were still closed, her heart filled with an emotion she dared not name. A hope she dared not have...

'Can you see it, Laura?' His voice was soft, so close to her, his breath warm on her cheek, as warm as the breeze wafting from the island of Capri. 'We're standing on the terrace in Amalfi. There's moonlight, and the sound of cicadas, and the sea far below. You're wearing something long and diaphanous, and your hair is like silk down your back. You're gazing up at me, and in your eyes is what is in mine. What we want of each other. What we feel for each other. What we're always going to feel for each other. All our days, Laura. All our nights.'

'Do you mean it—do you really mean it?'

Hope and fear mingled in her voice. She stared sightlessly at him, feeling only the contact of the tips of his fingers. Hoping and fearing so much.

He answered simply.

'Yes,' he said.

It was all he had to say.

Across her face a smile broke. Sudden. Unstoppable. Radiant like the sun. She threw her arms around him. Baggy ancient jumper, lank and straggling hair, unadorned face—she wrapped him close to her. So close.

As close as her heart.

He let her hug him. Knew she needed to know that she could do that—old Laura or new Laura, Laura the lie or Laura the truth. It didn't matter who she was, or what she was, she could hold him in her arms. Hold the man who, this very day, when he had restored her faith in herself again, would tell her that he loved her.

Because he did. He loved her. The truth of it blazed through him. As simple, as radiant as sunlight. Sunlight and the air he breathed. Certainty filled him, deep and abiding. And he knew, with the same deep, abiding certainty, that she loved him too.

She had just given him the surest proof of it. Trusting him enough to let her hug him. Embrace him.

Kiss him.

Deeply, sensuously, sensually. Lighting a fire in him that quickened instantly, feverishly. Demandingly. They clung to each other, desire leaping.

Then, with a groan, he drew back from her.

'I should let you go upstairs and beautify yourself, then take you away from here, dress you up, romance you and woo you, court you and pursue you. But I can't! I haven't the strength to hold back from you any longer. Let me love you now. Let me show you how I love you—*why* I love you!'

Her eyes were radiant as she gazed at him. Then she slipped her hand in his, her fingers embracing his tightly, urgently.

'Come,' she said.

And she took him to her bed.

And to her heart.

* * *

Something was dazzling Allesandro's closed eyes. Something bright and warm on his skin. He blinked his eyes open.

Sunlight was all around him. Flooding Laura's old fashioned bedroom, dazzling his eyes with dancing dust motes. Disbelievingly, Allesandro threw back the bedcovers and stood up. Without conscious volition he padded to the window, drawn by the dazzling brightness.

And just stared—amazed.

There was a footfall behind him, and then Laura was beside him, as naked as he was, pulling a sheet around them both.

'We'll shock the sheep,' she said humorously, wrapping her arm around his lean, warm waist.

Allesandro said something in Italian. Then he said it again in English.

'It's incredible,' he said. 'Fantastic!'

He was staring, just staring, out over the gardens of Wharton. Sunlight dazzled in the rain-dewed air, sparkling on the green lawns, lending a diamond brightness to the massed ranks of the multi-hued rhododendrons and rainbow azaleas, scorching colour on either flank, before the view dropped away to verdant woods and rolling fields beyond.

Laura reached forward to release the catch of the sash window and the upper half rattled down, letting in sweet, fresh air. She inhaled deeply. Allesandro looked at her.

'Now I understand why you love this place!' He put his arm around her shoulder, pulling her close. 'But no rubbish about holiday lets any more, understand? We'll live here ourselves!' There was decision in his voice. Then, as he leant out, resting his free arm on the top of the sash, a heavy raindrop fell from the eave onto his nose. He shook it away. 'But only in the summer,' he said, with equal decision. He stood back from the window, taking Laura with him, wrapped together as they were. As they always would be now.

'Show me the rest of the place,' he said. 'I want a total tour. Tell me everything you'll be doing to restore it.'

They dressed swiftly, and she showed him round the house—

arm in arm, hand in hand. Never letting him go. Happiness such
as she had never known was like a bright, shining star within her.
It would be there for ever now, she knew.

Because of the miracle. Not the miracle of her beauty, which
Allesandro had given her, but the much greater miracle. The
miracle of the love he had declared to her, of her body in his
arms, his in hers, now and for ever.

The greatest miracle of all.

EPILOGUE

THE rich haze of summer lay like a blessing on the gardens that lapped Wharton like a verdant multicoloured quilt. As she sat back in a padded garden chair, Laura looked at the house from their shady spot under the spreading oak, where the tea-tray rested on an ironwork table.

Happiness suffused her. The work on Wharton was finally complete, the old house lovingly restored. It still gave its sheltering grace to her, but it was no longer a refuge, but a warmly welcoming family home.

For my family…

She felt her heart catch. As if in silent understanding, Allesandro, relaxing in the dappled shade beside her, reached out to take her hand. On the other side of the table, snoozing peaceably, was her grandfather.

She and Allesandro had not told Tomaso about Stefano being gay, knowing he could not have dealt with the knowledge. Instead they had told him they had learnt he had been secretly in love with someone else—someone he could not marry—and that was why he had never married her mother. It had seemed to bring acceptance to her grandfather.

As for her Wharton grandparents—she hoped they, too, would have accepted that truth, accepted Tomaso as her grandfather and Allesandro as her husband.

And as for acceptance—well, Laura knew she and Allesandro

had had to do some of their own. Her eyes slid once more to Tomaso, and then softened.

Yes, he might have sought to tempt Allesandro with his resignation in order to get him to take her to Rome—however fruitlessly!—and, yes, he might even have tried to hurry things along by dropping hints to the tabloids. But—and it was a but that Laura now accepted—he had done it all for one reason and one reason only.

He did it for me, I know. He wanted me to have my chance with Allesandro, even if it meant seeking to manipulate the pair of us any way he could! He wanted me to have a chance of happiness and marriage!

Once more she heard in her memory her grandfather's words as he played chess with her—*'Always play to win.'*

An indulgent smile formed on her lips. Well, Tomaso had won, all right, but so had herself and Allesandro—they had won each other. Lovingly, she squeezed Allesandro's hand as he held hers in his. They were beyond her grandfather's wiles now.

As if on cue, Tomaso spoke.

'This is truly idyllic,' he announced, not opening his eyes. Then, without missing a blink, he continued, 'In weather like this, in summer, these gardens are unsurpassed. Ideal—just ideal, you know—for children.' He gave a rich sigh. 'Ah, I cannot tell you how much I *long* to see my great-grandchildren playing here…'

Saying nothing, only exchanging secret, private smiles, Laura and Allesandro rested their linked hands on the still invisible swell of her stomach.

They would tell Tomaso—of course they would!—but not quite yet.

Not *quite* yet.

For the moment, it was their joy alone.

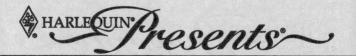

Don't miss favorite author

Michelle Reid's

next book, coming in May 2008,
brought to you only
by Harlequin Presents!

THE MARKONOS
BRIDE
#2723

Aristos is bittersweet for Louisa: here, she met
and married gorgeous Greek playboy Andreas
Markonos and produced a precious son. After
tragedy, Louisa was compelled to leave.
Five years later, she is back....

*Look out for more spectacular stories
from Michelle Reid, coming soon in 2008!*

REQUEST YOUR FREE BOOKS!

HARLEQUIN *Presents*®

2 FREE NOVELS
PLUS 2
FREE GIFTS!

PASSION • SEDUCTION
GUARANTEED

YES! Please send me 2 FREE Harlequin Presents® novels and my 2 FREE gifts (gifts are worth about $10). After receiving them, if I don't wish to receive any more books, I can return the shipping statement marked "cancel". If I don't cancel, I will receive 6 brand-new novels every month and be billed just $4.05 per book in the U.S. or $4.74 per book in Canada, plus 25¢ shipping and handling per book and applicable taxes, if any*. That's a savings of close to 15% off the cover price! I understand that accepting the 2 free books and gifts places me under no obligation to buy anything. I can always return a shipment and cancel at any time. Even if I never buy another book, the two free books and gifts are mine to keep forever.

106 HDN ERRW 306 HDN ERRL

Name	(PLEASE PRINT)	
Address		Apt. #
City	State/Prov.	Zip/Postal Code

Signature (if under 18, a parent or guardian must sign)

Mail to the Harlequin Reader Service:
IN U.S.A.: P.O. Box 1867, Buffalo, NY 14240-1867
IN CANADA: P.O. Box 609, Fort Erie, Ontario L2A 5X3

Not valid to current subscribers of Harlequin Presents books.

Want to try two free books from another line?
Call 1-800-873-8635 or visit www.morefreebooks.com.

* Terms and prices subject to change without notice. N.Y. residents add applicable sales tax. Canadian residents will be charged applicable provincial taxes and GST. This offer is limited to one order per household. All orders subject to approval. Credit or debit balances in a customer's account(s) may be offset by any other outstanding balance owed by or to the customer. Please allow 4 to 6 weeks for delivery. Offer available while quantities last.

Your Privacy: Harlequin Books is committed to protecting your privacy. Our Privacy Policy is available online at www.eHarlequin.com or upon request from the Reader Service. From time to time we make our lists of customers available to reputable third parties who may have a product or service of interest to you. If you would prefer we not share your name and address, please check here. ☐

HP08

HARLEQUIN *Presents*

**Be sure not to miss favorite
Harlequin Romance author**

Lucy Gordon

**in Harlequin Presents—
for one month only in May 2008!**

THE ITALIAN'S PASSIONATE REVENGE

#2726

Elise Carlton is wary of being a trophy wife—except
to rich, well-dressed and devastatingly handsome
Vincente Farnese. It is no coincidence that this dark
Italian has sought her out for seduction....

Coming in June 2008 in Harlequin Romance:

**The Italian's Cinderella Bride
by Lucy Gordon**